THE DESERTERS

THE
DESERTERS

Mathias Énard

translated by Charlotte Mandell

**A NEW DIRECTIONS
PAPERBOOK ORIGINAL**

Originally published in French as *Déserter* by Actes Sud in 2023.
Published by special arrangement with Actes Sud in conjunction
with their duly appointed agent, 2 Seas Literary Agency.

Manufactured in the United States of America
First published as New Directions Paperbook 1631 in 2025

Library of Congress Cataloging-in-Publication Data
Names: Énard, Mathias, 1972– author. | Mandell, Charlotte, translator.
Title: The deserters / Mathias Énard ; translated by Charlotte Mandell.
Other titles: Déserter. English
Description: New York : New Directions Publishing, 2025.
Identifiers: LCCN 2024059098 | ISBN 9780811239011 (paperback) |
ISBN 9780811239028 (ebook)
Subjects: LCGFT: Novels.
Classification: LCC PQ2705.N273 D46613 2025 |
DDC 843/.92—dc23/eng/20241212
LC record available at https://lccn.loc.gov/2024059098

2 4 6 8 10 9 7 5 3 1

New Directions Books are published for James Laughlin
by New Directions Publishing Corporation
80 Eighth Avenue, New York 10011

"And I pressed against their cool cheeks my cheek which now knew nothing but the kiss of the rifle butt."
— Francis Jammes, *Five Prayers for Wartime*

THE DESERTERS

I

He sets down his weapon and with difficulty takes off his boots, their smell (excrement, musty sweat) adds even more to his exhaustion. His fingers on the frayed laces are dry matchsticks, slightly burned in places; the nails are the same color as the boots, he'll have to scrape them with the tip of the knife to remove the filth, mud, dried blood, but later, he doesn't have the strength now; two toes, flesh and earth, emerge from the sock, they're fat spattered worms crawling out of a dark trunk, knotted at the ankle.

Suddenly he wonders, as he does every morning, as he does every evening, why these shoes stink of shit, it's inexplicable,

you can rinse them all you like in the pools of water you pass, rub them on tufts of grass that squeak, there's nothing to be done,

there aren't so many dogs or wild animals, not that many, in these rocky slopes sprinkled with holm oaks, pines, and thorn bushes where the rain leaves a fine light mud and the smell of flint, not shit, and it would be easy for him to believe it's the whole countryside that's mucid, from the sea and the hills of orange and then olive trees to the far mountains, these mountains, even himself, his own smell, not the smell of shoes, but he can't find an answer and throws the boots against the edge of the culvert that hides him from the path, a little higher up on the slope.

He lies down on his back on the gravel, sighs, the sky is purplish-blue, the gleams of the setting sun illumine the swift clouds from below, a canvas, a screen for a fireworks show. Spring is almost here and with it the often torrential rains that transform the mountains into tin cans pierced by bullets, powerful springs spouting from the slightest hollows, when the air smells of thyme and fruit tree flowers, white flakes scattered between the low walls by the violence of the downpour. All hell would break loose if it started raining now. But then at least it would wash his boots. His clogs, his uniform, his socks, the two pairs he owns are just as stiff, rigid, tattered. Betrayal begins with the body,

how long has it been since you last washed yourself?

four days spent walking near the ridges to avoid villages,

the last water you sprinkled yourself with smelled of gas and left your skin oily,

you're a long way from purity, alone under the sky ogling the comets.

Hunger forces him to straighten up and swallow without pleasure three military biscuits, the last ones, hard brown slabs, no doubt a mixture of sawdust and horse glue; for an instant he curses the war and soldiers,

you're still one of them, you still carry weapons, ammunition, and memories of war,

you could hide your gun and cartridges somewhere and become a beggar, leave the knife too, beggars have no daggers,

the boots that stink of shit and set off barefoot,

the jacket with its color of misery and go bare-chested,

meal over he empties his flask and plays at pissing as far as possible toward the valley.

He lies down again, this time right up against the wall of the slope, the bottom part of his bag under his head; he is invisible in the shadow, never mind the little critters (red spiders, tiny scorpions, centipedes with teeth as sharp as remorse) that will gambol on his chest, slide across his almost shaven skull, walk over his beard as rough as a bramble bush. The rifle leaning against him, the butt under his shoulder, muzzle toward his feet. Rolled up in the piece of oiled canvas that serves as blanket and roof.

The mountain rustles; a little wind overtakes the summits, descending into the combe and vibrating between the bushes; the cries of the stars are chilling. There are no more clouds, it won't rain tonight.

Angel, my holy guardian, protector of my body and soul, forgive me for all the sins committed on this day and deliver me from the works of the enemy, despite the warmth of the prayer the night remains a beast fed on anguish, a beast with breath of blood, cities in ruins full of mothers brandishing the mutilated corpses of their children faced with scruffy hyenas that will torture them, then leave them naked, dirty, their nipples torn with teeth under the eyes of their brothers raped in turn with truncheons, terror stretched over the country, plague, hatred, and darkness, this darkness that always envelops you and urges you toward cowardice and treason. Flight and desertion. How much time is there left to walk? The border is a few days from here, beyond the mountains that will soon become hills of red earth, planted with olive trees. It will be difficult to hide. Many villages, towns, farmers, soldiers,

you know the region,

you are home here,

no one will help a deserter,

you'll reach the house in the mountain tomorrow,

the cabin, the hovel, you'll take refuge there for a little while,

the cabin will protect you with its childhood,

you'll be caressed with its memories,

sometimes sleep comes by surprise like the bullet of a marksman lying in ambush.

II

I have to go back over what happened over twenty years ago, on September 11, 2001, near Potsdam on the Havel, on board the cruise boat, a little river liner christened with the fine pompous name *Beethoven*.

Summer seemed to be wavering. The willows were still green, the days still warm, but a freezing fog would rise from the river before dawn and immense clouds seemed to be gliding over us, from the distant Baltic.

Our floating hotel had left Köpenick east of Berlin very early in the morning, on Monday. Maja was always alert, spry. She would go up to the top deck to walk, a stroll between showers, deck chairs, and deck games. The green domes and golden spire of the Berlin cathedral captivated her, from afar, when we arrived. She was imagining, she said, all the little gilt angels leaving their stone prison to fly off into a cloud of acanthus leaves blown by the sun.

The water of the Spree was sometimes a dull, dark blue, sometimes a glowing green. During the preceding weeks, all of Germany had been rocked by storms; their aftermaths swelled the Havel and the Spree, which usually were quite low at summer's end.

We navigated through the swirling water.

I remember the confluence of the Spree, the little wooded islands, the salt light that dusted the tall dark poplars and the muddy stream of the canal that the ship's wake mixed with the polished water of the river.

Maja and I were sitting in canvas chairs, in the sun on the aft deck, astern as one should say, and we were watching as everything fled: the landscape opened up as if the ship's prow were spreading wide the green substance of leaves.

We were celebrating (a few months late) the tenth anniversary of Paul's radical reform of the Institute, as well as paying homage to the founder himself. Or, more precisely, we were celebrating the tenth anniversary of the Institute's "unification," in Spring 1991, and the fortieth anniversary of its creation in 1961. But mostly we were celebrating Paul's work as a whole. I don't think anyone was missing—among the historical ones, the ones from the East, they were all there; almost all of the new members, the colleagues from Berlin and elsewhere, were in attendance. Some, including Linden Pawley, Robert Kant, and a few of the French scholars, even came from abroad. This floating conference was called the "Paul Heudeber Days"; two sessions a day were scheduled: number theory and algebraic topology, along with one discussion of the history of mathematics in which I was slated to take part.

The only person absent was Paul himself.

Maja had just celebrated her eighty-third birthday.

Maja drank liters of tea.

Maja was cheerful and sad and silent and talkative.

We all knew she had nothing to do there, on board the *Beethoven* for a math conference; we all knew she was indispensable to it.

Prof. Dr. Paul Heudeber
Elsa-Brändström-Str. 32
1100 Berlin Pankow
RDA

Maja Scharnhorst
Heussallee 33
5300 Bonn 1

Sunday, September 1, 1968

Maja Maja Maja

Let's take away the possessive: love stripped bare.

It grew in absence and night: the lack of you is a source. A body, a ring—you are the seal of all things, unique. Your distance brings the infinite close. You alone allow me to hide myself from time, from evil, from the tides of melancholy. I wonder what there was of my youth, when I hear its cries.

I block my ears with clever calculations.

I hurtle over surfaces over which no one has ever trod.

I remember September 1938. Fire smoldered in iron; our fire in irons.

We remained standing faced with the ruins to come.

We held on, connected to each other by the force of memory.

Just as we hold firm today, in fear and hope faced with the world in front of us.

Irina has just turned seventeen, barely the blink of an eye for a star.

I can't wait for you to come back.

I'll make some concessions; I'll visit you in the West.

I've read your beautiful text, in that horrible journal, on the Prague affair.

I miss our clashes.

I leave Tuesday for Moscow, a conference.

I wonder how they can think during these dangerous times, over there.

Moscow of thick towers and comrades.

Write to me.

To say "love and kisses" says very little.

Paul

Most people traveling on trains prefer to sit facing forward.

A historian is someone who has chosen not to sit facing forward.

A historian of the sciences is a historian who, facing backwards, toward the rear, unlike most historians does not look out the window.

A historian of mathematics is a historian of the sciences who, facing backwards, eyes closed, tries to demonstrate that Arabs invented trains.

No one laughed.

It should be said that I was the only historian in the conference. All the others were mathematicians, physicists, or, worse, logicians. All facing forward. Looking toward innovation, invention, discovery. I was the only one who was less interested in the glorious demonstrations and inventions of tomorrow than in the sweet meanderings of the past. Meanderings of the past that project their light to the furthest limits of the future, and I felt, during this "Paul Heudeber Days" colloquium on the Havel, that this audience of scholars would only listen to my talk on Nasir al-Din Tusi and irrational numbers with a suitable respect for the circumstances, full of consideration for me and my mother, who despite her age wouldn't miss a second of the lectures, between her strolls on the deck.

Maja was the source of the idea for this fluvial conference; I think I remember that Jürgen Thiele, the general secretary, had suggested "an afternoon walk on the Spree or the Havel" at the end of the conference, which was initially supposed to take place at the Institute in Berlin; she'd made a face, the Spree or the Havel, it's still Berlin at best, Brandenburg at worst, why not the Danube, and Jürgen Thiele had looked surprised, the Danube, but that's very far away, and I imagine Maja had burst out laughing, OK, go with the Havel, but at least the whole conference should be on a boat, and Jürgen Thiele was very embarrassed (he told me later) since he didn't want to refuse my mother anything for these days of homage but he had limited funds—the business of the river conference continued to seem absurd to him, a whim of old age.

Nevertheless, Thiele had the surprise of receiving two letters on the same day, a few weeks before the call to participate in the "Days" was published: one informed him that the mathematics faculty at the University of Potsdam was offering to coorganize the "Paul Heudeber Days" with our Institute, and the other that the Georg Cantor Foundation was granting (without any solicitation on Thiele's part) an enormous subsidy that made possible its river setting (aberrant though it was, he thought without speaking).

Paul's tragic death a few years ago had deeply affected the scientific community; everyone was eager to participate, and even though most of the organizers (Jürgen Thiele especially) didn't know the reason for Maja's wish, no one wanted to disappoint her. These two letters arrived in the nick of time, and Jürgen could only suspect, rightly no doubt, that Maja had picked up her pen or telephone: although theoretically retired from politics ever since the 1998 federal elections, she still had the power to attract "benevolent attention" to nascent projects. The money from the Georg Cantor Foundation was welcome; Jürgen Thiele, as coorganizer, got in touch with the University of Potsdam, which was celebrating its tenth anniversary, Paul having helped found it: many of its math professors had been his students.

The "Paul Heudeber Days," then, would take place on the Havel, on board a cruise ship capable of hosting, in its conference room, the fifty or so attendees; participants from outside of Berlin were mostly put up at a hotel opposite Peacock Island, or Pfaueninsel, located technically in Wannsee—a hotel with a medieval or alpine inn name, the White Owl, an inn Maja assured me (I wondered how she could be so sure) had existed at least since the sixteenth century, but whose present building—Doric columns supporting a monumental balcony, windows with green shutters, climbing roses, like in a fairytale, softening the facade with their countless flowers, all dark red, veering to black—had been rebuilt by Karl

Schinkel in the first third of the nineteenth century. The White Owl was lost in the middle of the forest on the edge of an immense lake crossed by the Havel. Only the keynote speakers and other conference VIPs were put up on board the *Beethoven*, since there weren't many cabins; daytime "sailings," however, were open to everyone: Potsdam–Elbe on Wednesday, a day of actual homage, centered on Paul's work, then Peacock Island–Köpenick via Spandau on Thursday to close the festivities. Only a few prestigious guests had arrived on Sunday to take advantage of the boat's "presailing" from Köpenick to Wannsee, and then enjoy an additional cruise day through Berlin on Monday.

Jürgen Thiele was full of empathy, confusion, and goodwill. Even though he was still the Institute's general secretary, Thiele took on this responsibility only out of loyalty to Paul, whose student he had been thirty years before; he was the first to admit that he was tired of organizing, getting things ready, giving orders — even arranging a Christmas lunch throws me into a panic, he confessed. So a conference with fifty people, imagine! The University of Potsdam had assigned him a coorganizer, a young graduate student writing her doctoral thesis on number theory named Alma Sejdić, who was trying to demonstrate a corollary to Paul's First Conjecture. This addition turned out to be as disastrous as it was hilarious: instead of adding to each other, these two forces seemed either to be pointlessly combining, or canceling each other out. Things forgotten were forgotten twice, blunders doubled. It was like a drawing made by two ballpoint pens attached with a rubber band: parallel lines never joining, despite all their efforts, constrained by Euclid himself.

Jürgen Thiele must have mustered all his diplomacy to avoid vexing the University of Potsdam, which didn't understand why it had to finance, a few kilometers from its campus, the rental of a *luxury* river boat — but Jürgen Thiele had pulled from his sleeve the grant from the Georg Cantor Foundation, and everyone found the idea of a floating conference *thrilling*.

And so, after a few months of this ballet in chaos, we landed,

Maja and I, as planned, on Sunday, September 9, in Köpenick, in the company of Linden Pawley, whose flight from New York had set down in Tegel that very morning, the inevitable Robert Kant of Cambridge, and Jürgen Thiele—there were indeed five luxury cabins all prepared for us.

III

Every morning since he left, the cold has awakened him just before dawn. He is shivering. No sudden movements, so that the dew, dark pearls on the canvas, doesn't stream down. Patiently, by folding his tent into a furrow, he manages to fill his flask with a few ounces of this icy dawn sweat to drink, which will be his only morning meal.

He sets off, once his reluctant feet are wrapped in the wretched green spongy knit, still wet, in the direction of destiny, north, for chaos and oblivion must be named. Once again he hesitates to leave the rifle behind, it's heavy, and its strap is uncomfortable, too short ever since he cut it to make a belt from it, with the knife that's still so sharp, yet another sign of a dangerous solitude, drunk with blood, he doesn't think anymore, he's already walking when the first rays of sun root out the shadows from the rocks. These needles of light animate the sparrows and warblers and titmice, and the movements of their wings follow the train of the song of morning.

If he's thinking so much about birds, if he's so caught up in their presence and song, it's because they rouse hunger in him—it would be so easy to hide out, nose to the wind, with the rifle, to wait for one of those little feathered creatures to betray itself, to shoot and eat it, but the power of the weapon of war would leave nothing but feathers, the sound of gunfire would echo far into the hills, and even if a fat pheasant or partridge stumbled into his line of sight, it would have to be cooked, and he has no intention of interrupting his march for long or revealing himself with fire or smoke.

He has resolved to reach the house.

You could find it even on a moonless night,
the cabin,

feel it advancing in the daylight between the holm oaks, scattered by the dryness; a few lentiscs are sheltering among the rocks, freeing as the walker passes their medicinal smell, from some far-off pharmacy; he looks out for the fresh wild basil that spring causes to proliferate in the mountains and chews for a long time on a sprig, bitter, acidic, peppery—arbutus berries still survive in winter like forgotten Christmas decorations, coarse and red, they taste like overripe strawberries, bland as oblivion.

These fruits are tiny stars, planets in arm's reach,

little moons reddened by desire and cunning,

the sun, at each step, illumines the petals of the dogwood flowers, their bright yellow is dimmed by no leaf, on their still-bare branches the first fissure in winter opens up by magic.

He walks like the last man, in the restless rustling of the mountain.

He envies the black spots of airplanes or distant birds of prey.

Overcome by remembering, ass on a rock—one of those stones veering to blue-gray, which warm up quickly in the sun and smell of metal and gunflint, smooth as they are hard: was there an initial shudder, a harsh wind, premise of the logic of brutality, a bellow preceding the sovereign rutting of war, he thinks not,

it's the surprise that sat you down there,

soon the black snakes will emerge from their holes and the males will set out in search of females,

he unlaces his boots, undoes the knots and takes them off. The leather is gnawed away by wear, water, and cold. The smell of shit hasn't left him. His hands are rough; his white palm is starred with darker callouses, stiff from squeezing wooden handles for too long. His tobacco-stained fingers end in yellowing nails streaked with black filth, you can see the outline of veins, in his thumb and along his wrist; his cheeks are coarse with a patchy beard, his hair is greasy, in clumps, stuck together in darker strands with dried blood,

you'll reach the house before nightfall,

the house, the cabin, the shack—it rests deep in his memories and hopes. Childhood country cairn. At the edge of the enemy lines. High enough in the mountain so that no one will venture there. Concealed enough from the mountain people so that he can seclude himself there. For a while. The roof might be partly collapsed, the cypress pillars, round, still gleaming, will stand alone, without tiles, between the uneven stones. The very low door. The front porch, its wooden struts reminiscent of the arms of the Father, its two stone posts, unevenly squared, the columns of the temple of a brutal God. The facade of unplastered quarried stone. The roof made of old yellow clay tiles,

you can sculpt faces with the knife in the pillars like you used to,
you're so hungry it's frightening,
you're hungry down to the roots of your hair,
imagining the little grill in the cabin's porch and a fowl crackling
on the embers makes him writhe in raging pain,
you are thirsty,
he drains his metal flask. The lovely March sun is tinted orange.
A wind is blowing from the sea,
you walk forward,
you must move forward even if you stumble a little, clumsy
with dizziness. He lets thoughts fly away as soon as they're born.
He chases them away with his feet, makes them flee by walking.
He transmits his thoughts to his boots, scattering them in the
pebbles. Then silence inside, until the return of the great fixed
star of hunger.
The treachery of illusion, the perfume of spring returning.
The sea, its violet plains fringed with white.
So high up in the mountain the sea is nothing but a threatening
line, a horizon of pain.
His feverishness distorts distance: the more he walks, the further away the house recedes.
You're making too much noise,
you shouldn't trust the scree looming over the cabin,
lie down in the sunset and observe strange movements—abandoned dogs made feral by war, deserters, villagers, distant cousins,
all of them, far from their relics, on the path to the hermitage, to
escape suffering, to be done with the long Lent of blood,
Spring suddenly takes his breath away. A spring of the beating
of wings, of flowers on rocks, of thorn bushes, of white and blue
rosemary, of the buzzing of the beetles' elytra—the track he was
following sloped down a few dozen meters to the sea; he takes
off his clothes stiff with filth, stained with grease and dried blood,
finds himself bare-chested licked by the sea breeze and blinded by
the power of the sun whose burning heat he feels on his shoulders,
on the long scar streaking across his back, before the bag's cloth

covers it. Tired of the too-short gun strap, he takes his weapon in his arms like a hunter, his left hand on the stock, his right on the grip the way you grasp a fowl's neck, firmly, casually; the breech is open, he sees the brass of a cartridge case in the cartridge, once again he wants to get rid of the object of misfortune,

it's heavier than a child in your arms,

you should abandon it, hide it there in a bush, a few hours' walk from the cabin,

he plays with the well-oiled breech, impossible to get rid of it,

Fate in front of you and all these things, the remains, the traces, and the great mourning of the future,

you'll be what the Lord wants,

force or forgiveness, nothing, like this yellow spider under your boot, crushed despite its power for death, crushed despite its sting, all that we don't know about ourselves, we bend beneath the world of yesterday, we bend beneath our sins, we bend beneath the prospect of the next day, our Father give us this day our daily oblivion, in the too-numerous steps that wear down our soul, yard after yard, path after path, track after track, this sudden emotion comes from nearby—one day walking—from the village below, halfway up the slope, where the orange trees are little by little invading the plains, where the olive trees make themselves scarce on the terraces with their stone walls, where a few towers appear among the houses with gentle arches, with their broken domes between the green medlar trees, lit up with orange fruit in June, among the noble fig trees bent with age whose figs hum with insects in autumn, just as the trellis shaded the terrace in front of the father's house, a wine was pressed there that quickly stung the tongue, purple, troubling and intoxicating—the green demijohns, woven round with straw, piled up in the darkest, coolest recesses, until they were cleaned in September to receive the new vintage, and the red and black clouds of tannin clinging there inside their glass shoulders were scrubbed away with a metal bottle brush,

you'll have to hide, they must be looking for you,

you mustn't come across anyone, conceal yourself from men and beasts, from shepherds and dogs, swallow your own name,

the closer your footsteps bring you to the cabin, to the mountain house, the greater the danger grows, in the village everyone
knows, no doubt, rumors swell like the war itself, everyone knows,
or thinks they know,

the afternoon swells like thirst and reddens like hunger.

He pauses in the shade of a holm oak. He sits down on a root.
The sun drenches the valley in front of him. He dreams of rain.
He shakes his flask over his tongue one more time. He unties his
shoes, hesitates to take them off, he's so tired he won't put them
back on if he removes them. The smell seems to have disappeared
for an instant but returns, even stronger, unexpectedly,

you stink of blood and shit,

you stink of sleep and hunger,

a child could kill you with one punch,

he counts the days since he left the city. Since his flight from the
barracks. Four days since he launched the vehicle into the ravine,

you've traveled almost a hundred kilometers on foot in the
mountain,

the holm oak's root is hard under your buttocks,

your bent knees hurt,

he leans against the black trunk, stretches out his legs, gazes
into the valley (almond trees, hazelnut trees, prickly pear trees) he
knows so well. He worked these terraces, weeded around the trees,
removed countless stones. The sun that he knows. The fringe of
sea beyond the hills that he knows. The fear that he carries with
him. That black smoke on the horizon marks the beginning of
the enemy territory. There, only just. The remains of the enemy
territory as it's reduced from shell to shell.

At the next turn in the path, when he passes the old retention
basin for the stream, dried up now, he'll be two hours' walk from
the house. He'll reach it almost an hour before sunset,

you know where you'll take cover,

behind the big rock and make sure without being seen that no
one's hanging around the cabin. Behind the rock and observe.
Observe the last insects in the twilight. Listen to the birds and
stones in the twilight.

He takes out the knife. The blade is as gray as it is blue. He dreams of a hare, leaping out of a hollow, suddenly within reach of the dagger. He draws a cross on the tree root. A short thin cross. A sign. He would have been capable of drinking the warm blood of that hare if it had appeared, he's so thirsty,

you're feverish like those areas in your memory,

for hours he's been searching for an orange tree or even a lemon tree on whose branches there might still be a few forgotten fruits. Opposite the cabin is an immense lemon tree planted by his grandfather that bears (or rather bore, it's been a long time since he saw it last) dozens of juicy yellow fruits, with thick skins, which leave on your hands a scent of linen and flowers, a perfume of purity, purity pleases the Lord,

there's also an orange tree, they used to weave crowns from its flowers for weddings,

you're the least pure of creatures,

he finds the strength to start off again, with his painful knees, his thighs hard as rocks, his scratched feet; the further away the war gets the more his body falls to pieces, an old mechanism that only habit kept functioning. He's almost incapable of climbing the few kilometers still separating him from the cabin, from the house, from the purple mists and hollows of clouds. It's his rifle that carries him and guides him, the immense needle of a magic compass, the wand of a douser of death,

you can hardly walk, you're staggering, you're making too much noise,

he chases away the tiny flies that pursue him and always catch up with him. The sun burns his skin that emerged fragile from the cold of war, he's a lizard revived by warmth; everything in him is stretched between fear and exhaustion.

His footsteps suddenly (rolling stones, quivering branches, the sound of wings) startle a pigeon a few meters away. He snaps the breech closed to arm the rifle and shoulders it—he doesn't fire,

you're too close to the villages, mustn't attract the attention of a shepherd who might be passing by, he watches the bird disappear behind a copse of holm oaks to find its companion,

these fowl always travel in pairs,

they're the inseparable couple of the mountain, the inevitable ones of spring, along with the nightingales. He engages the gun's safety. On top of the pass between those two hills dotted with rocks the cabin will come into sight. He observes the clouds amassing suddenly gray over the line of the sea. A cloud veils the sun. The wind transforms the drops of sweat on his shoulders and chest into as many frozen pins and needles. He had forgotten the dexterity of the cold—he forces himself to pause to put his jacket back on, with pain and dread, it has become stiff with all the fluids filling its fibers,

you stink of the slaughterhouse, that's the stench you reek of, the stench of guts and the stream of water over blackened tiles,

a stench of meat,

he runs his left hand over his face, feels the roughness of his beard, like a kind of bark. The sun's disappearance signifies the return of altitude as much as of shadow: he is shivering. Behind him, a little further down, a cottony mist is spreading between folds in the hills, a white fog on red earth, the sea has disappeared. Steel eats away at the horizon. He launches all his strength onto the rocks to cross them, onto the slopes to climb them. The pass is bellowing, the pass is freezing his face. The wind flattens his face and shoulders. He clings to his rifle and leans forward. Stumble by stumble he reaches the shelter of a rock, a few dozen meters lower down. He leans against it,

the house is down below on your right,

he observes, there is the roof of tiles more yellow than red, a single-sloping roof, leaning against the mountain in the back, he glimpses the porch, the short chimney, the partition wall made of quarried stone, the low walls around the abandoned garden, not an animal in sight, in the distance a raptor is spiraling, a tiny solitary spot in the now milky sky, the paddock on the right of the garden is empty, the tall almond tree in front of the house has no leaves yet, the lemon tree is green with that solemn green of citrus trees, eternal, a sepulchral green with yellow glints in the shifting light of the absent sun, no smoke is rising from the chimney, an odor of thyme and snow floats in the air,

if you had binoculars, you'd search for traces,

signs of someone's presence, shepherds, farmers, refugees, creatures, angels, demons,

there's just the brief hesitant plain that breaks as it nears the sea, only the wind crossing the walls can be heard, his back to the rock hands around his knees the rifle on his right bag at his feet like a motionless dog he waits, he waits for the time he planned for, the two hours left before the darkest part of the night, reassured by the presence of the cabin, by the lemons in the lemon tree, by the old orange tree invisible to him next to the hazelnut tree beyond the cabin to the right of the wall,

all urgency abolished by the sudden presence of childhood,

wingbeat by wingbeat,

wandering backwards,

you wait for the apparition, Lord thy invisible face, you wait for Sirius, you wait for Orion, you wait for thy face, Lord,

your ass is frozen by the scraps of winter the mountain always harbors,

the mountain preserves winter, the orange and lemon trees preserve winter—December fruits are still hanging from the branches when the flowers open in April, he forces his eyes into the settling twilight, he forces his gaze, he sees nothing, not one movement, not one shadow aside from that of the almond tree that's growing, and of the shack that's growing, a blackbird is singing in the evening, a blackbird Lord one of thy creatures is singing of thy glory, all creatures sing thy glory, hope brews in his chest, it's the presence of the shack and the voice of the blackbird,

hope Lord is born from thee,

you will find a little childhood and rest in the shack,

the shack where you used to go with your father, where your father used to go with his father, used to grow things, gather things, grow things, the house is in front of your eyes and with no movement, no presence, it's night now or almost, the bird's voice has fallen silent, he'll go down to the cabin, the shack, the house whatever name it's given,

you limp, stumble, the bag and rifle are heavy,

the path uncoils like a snake on the mountainside, no more stars in the sky and the wind, the wind is always at war.

IV

Isolation, the events that weighed over 2021, the war, so close, so present and so sudden: so many waves that push me toward the reefs. I've spent my adult life writing, talking and writing, and today, when I've just celebrated my seventieth birthday, for the first time it's my own life I'm narrating. How Paul's life is reflected in it, and Maja's; the numbers frighten me, the dates, the places; it's much easier for me to hold forth on the algebra of Khayyam or the discoveries of Nasir al-Din Tusi in the thirteenth century than to break the walls erected between myself and myself by years of modesty. Modesty or something else. Even after being dead for twenty-five years, Paul is still here. Maja too. She left us in 2005 at the age of eighty-seven. The Chancellor's wife was at her funeral, the President was at her funeral, hundreds of people I didn't know were at her funeral.

When a generation seems to be vanishing, affluence at funerals increases.

An effect of rarity.

Mourning is a form of endless presence. Images, perfumes, tastes, dreams.

The river, a long patience.

Maja and I used to look at the trees on the banks fleeing into the distance.

I still cherish a green sweetness from those hours.

The strange machicolations and the red roof of the Grunewald Tower.

The seeming ease of the current.

Maja, in a chaise longue, cup of tea in hand.

The sun rising over Berlin.

I was born in 1951, in a clinic in the American sector near the Botanical Garden. My parents were thirty-three. Paul was finishing up writing his accreditation thesis while teaching algebra at Humboldt University. Maja was still very politically active and was working with Franz Dahlem, after his party, the Social Democrat Party, had merged with the German Communist Party to form the Unified Socialist Party in the Soviet Occupation Zone. The Democratic Republic of Germany was just two years old; two years later all Maja's hope, already chipped away by the blockade of Berlin, collided with the riots of June 1953; she moved without my father to the West (they were never married) and pursued her political career with Willy Brandt.

Paul defended his thesis and obtained his first post at the Academy of Sciences in Berlin just when intellectuals were starting to flee the GDR. The work entitled *The Ettersberg Conjectures, Mathematical Elegies*, was one of the first books published by the Academy's press at the end of 1947. It was comprised of studies Paul Heudeber wrote during his captivity in Buchenwald between 1940 and 1946. Venerated today as a treasure by scientific and literary communities, the *Conjectures* was reprinted only once in East Germany, in 1973 (in a purely mathematical version, without the poems, the corollaries, the commentaries on camp life) and it wasn't until 1991 that the Akademie Verlag reprinted the original version, augmented by Paul with fragments he himself had left out of the first publication (mainly love poems to Maja written between 1937 and 1947). It's this version, under the title *The Buchenwald Conjectures*, translated into English by Robert Kant in Cambridge, that became known all over the world, the only math book to have known relative success, so much so that the publishers, who thought this success could be even greater, suggested to Paul that he authorize an exclusively "literary" version, without the mathematical expositions, which he of course refused until his death.

Robert Kant's contribution to the 2001 conference (a contribution he was revising with us during the river journey through Berlin) had to do with the first conjecture, on the circumstances of the birth of this extraordinary project, in the heart of the extreme violence of the concentration camp, and on the way Paul Heudeber launched this imaginary dialogue, from his barracks, with the mathematicians of previous generations: the first conjecture (hence the first chapter) deals with the theorems of David Hilbert; the second is devoted to Paul's famous demonstration of the twin prime conjecture, and so on.

Robert Kant argued that the originality of Paul's text—apart from its inarguably literary quality, its considerations on the Revolution, its obscure passages, its dark poetry—stems from its scientific radicality: from the intersection, in the heart of the twentieth century, of historical despair with mathematical hope.

Those days appeared to me under the sign of Saturn: they were bathed in a profound melancholy. The proximity of Maja radiated at once the pleasure of her presence and the pain of the imminence of her death, the last glints of the sun of my mother's life. After his tragic death in 1995, Paul still remained extremely close, his body transformed into language, his name uttered like an incantation a hundred times a day by the conference participants. The river was the very expression of this melancholy, its most beautiful metaphor: what we watch disappear, what flees to the great unknown producing a green, fluid, iridescent, endless beauty, always present and never the same. Starting Monday, on the Havel between Spandau and Potsdam, this melancholy glued me to my deck chair, with the sun.

Maja was next to me, she never stopped talking, as usual; I realized that this voice, which floated off into the middle of the river, had accompanied me all my life and that it was going to fade away, and that it was going to fade away soon.

That plunged me into a child's sadness.

Maja and Paul already had their names in all the history books; we had just changed centuries, millennia; the river was ridding the continent of its waste, its impurities; it was flinging all our dark materials into the Elbe, to add them to the shadows of the north.

The present was swaying, from one foot to the other, like someone hearing alluring music and wondering whether to dance.

All the threads of History seemed gathered together in a single hand.

Dinner on Monday, once the boat was moored at the dock in front of the White Owl inn, in the middle of the forest, opposite Peacock Island, and in the bluish calm of Wannsee Lake, was above all a dress rehearsal for the opening of the conference the next morning. The students Jürgen had recruited to help organize the conference, we learned, would be there at eight o'clock to welcome the participants, who would then receive their badges, their programs, their cardboard file folders from the Institute containing a notepad, a wooden pencil, some information on the "Paul Heudeber Days," some brochures advertising the main sponsors, and a tourist map of the city of Potsdam and the neighborhood of Wannsee.

I had been asked (in a more personal than scientific capacity, obviously) to choose a photo of Paul for the program. I had vacillated for a long time, taken out the albums and moved dozens of photos around, private or public images, taken by lenses of Praktica or Pentacon cameras from East Germany, some photos surrounded by an embellished white border: New Year's Eves in the apartment on the Elsa-Brändström-Strasse in Pankow, their colors very red, at once faded and saturated; photos of me as a schoolgirl, photos of Maja and me, travel photos in Prague, a strange picture of Fidel Castro in Berlin with, who knows what he was doing there, Paul in the background, smiling and wearing a tie; photos in the company of President Honecker at the medal ceremony, images with unknown officials at the Science Institute, and finally the portrait I'd ended up choosing: Paul smiling, just over thirty-five, tieless, in shirtsleeves, holding a piece of chalk in front of a blackboard on which the viewer can see an elaboration of the Riemann zeta function and other equations having to do with prime numbers. Maja remembered this photo, which she had taken at Humboldt University at the very beginning of the 1950s.

Going over all these images, these memories, had plunged me into a joyful, almost sweet sadness, the same as the one I feel today, softened by twenty years of distance.

Berlin is blanketed in silence; the white masks that used to haunt Schlossstrasse have disappeared. The plague atmosphere, the smell of fear and disinfectant that used to nauseate me, has vanished, suddenly everyone has only the word "war" in their mouths. The pleasure I found in solitude fades away. The pervading confusion cracks the walls of my apartment.

Reading and transcribing the correspondence between Maja and Paul delights and exhausts me at the same time. No matter how much I try to think like a historian, to see these letters as a source, like any other source, to read over three thousand missives, written between 1945 and 1995, while outside, everything is being extinguished in an endless dry cough or in the echo of gunfire, shifts me in time—this journey is wearing me out. Berlin today looks very pale next to this sun. This passion is too bright. Paul wanted to project all the light possible on his love to chase away its shadows. He removed it from the imperfection of the flesh. He made it into an object of the soul. He devoted sixty years of his life to it, between his meeting with Maja in 1938 and his death, sixty years of passion. And it's up to me to dismantle this machine, to refute this theorem, to patiently dissect this animal.

It's up to me to place the grimace of death on the face of the icon.

V

He bites into the orange as if it were an apple, the juice runs down, follows the curves of his chin, he takes another bite, his thirst is inside his hunger like a ball, he chews, it's bitter, acidic, and sweet, it's an incredible pleasure, he almost chokes, he almost swallows the orange, regurgitates it, seizes another, in the almost total darkness that follows dusk, the perfume of the tree and the sudden cold that overwhelms him despite the joy.

He puts four oranges into his bag,

you'll go into the shack, the door is the same, the same dark wood, the same rusty metal bolt, the chain isn't on the lock, it's hanging down, the padlock open hanging from the lintel,

no sign of violence,

no light inside,

he maneuvers the cast iron bolt, the smell submerges him, the smell of burnt almond wood, of the past, of ashes, of rosemary, of damp walls,

the rock in the back of the cabin used to sweat dew sometimes in winter the way an icon sweats oil, you'll be fine here despite the cold,

an old wicker basket is full of almonds, a bunch of dried sage is hanging on the white wall, above the whitewashed stone benches, which serve as cupboards, chairs, armchairs, and beds; the wooden table is ancient, he sits down on the bench, back against the wall in the dark, some pale light is still outlined on the threshold despite the cloudy night, he breathes in the shadow, inhales the refuge.

Then he places the rifle in the corner of the house, on the bench; he keeps the knife on his belt; he takes down a few branches of dried rosemary, some pieces of wood, almond and holm oak, puts them in the fireplace, you're no longer afraid they'll glimpse the fire in the distance, smell the smoke,

he strikes a light,

the rosemary seems to hesitate an instant, its leaves, tiny spears, curl up, sweat, sputter, and catch fire, their light is suddenly blinding, the white flames attack the almond and holm oak wood. He sat down on the ground in front of the fire, hypnotized by the heat, warmed by memory, not everything has disappeared with the war, not everything is dead, the cabin and memory are still here and he falls asleep sitting there, chin on his chest, hands on his stomach, fingers interlaced as if he were praying,

Lord thou art in me, Lord I feel thy heat, it comes from the past, it is in dream, in the caress of dream and fire,

daylight surprises him on the wide stone bench, not remembering lying down on it, he opens one eye onto the silence, he hasn't even taken off his boots, hasn't even taken off his jacket, he seizes one of the oranges that he put on the table, peels it gently with the knife, the skin reminds him of human skin, he eats the orange section by section, it is sour and juicy, cold. He goes outside; sleep sticks to his eyes, daylight is there, the sun in its place under a veil of clouds, the trees, his father's old vegetable garden, terraced like a balcony on the slope, with the purple diadem of the sea in the distance in front of the red hills, the villages, the olive trees, the black smoke of war, and behind him the great steel shoulder of the mountains. The air is perfumed with insects. He walks over to the well, the spring in a hollow of rock that feeds the well, the water source was their only wealth, the cement drainage grooves leaving from there to irrigate the lands below—the war has turned the terraces wild, they are taken over by thistle, myrtle, heather with its tiny white flowers. He wipes away the rocks hiding the thick rusty metal lid and lifts it—a spider flees, a black glint reveals the presence of water, he sprinkles himself with it, it is freezing, he plunges his whole head into it, it's like burying his face in snow, he stands up, takes off his jacket, pants, socks, he is naked, shivering, he splashes himself with some more freezing water, seizes a clay pitcher with a broken handle, fills it and empties it over his head while he shivers, he rubs his face to get rid of the congealed blood and filth, he has no soap, he clumsily rubs his armpits, genitals,

your father used to wash you at the spring, you were cold and afraid of getting beaten if you moved, if you tried to escape the freezing water the blows would rain down, blows and insults,

he pours water on his socks next, then his jacket and pants, then his underwear, removing as much dirt as he can by rubbing them against each other, a blackish juice flows from the fabric, he washes the clothes for a long time, before placing them in the sun on the rock near the porch, he sits down, bare-assed, on a rock, the wind has fallen, the clouds have disappeared, the sun is warm—when a noise reaches him, bird or branch, he stiffens,

you'd look smart taken by surprise stark naked like that,

but taken by surprise by whom, by what, by a stray dog, a wolf, he's never seen a wolf, those eyes that shine in the night, those eyes that growl before ripping your throat open,

you'd better get your rifle,

there's something childlike in nudity, childlike, soldierlike or prisonlike,

all those people you've seen naked now here you are naked in turn but in solitude,

the sudden breeze rises again,

that will dry your kit faster now,

he takes refuge inside the cabin, he'd like to find a piece of mirror to look at himself but there's nothing in the bench's large chests, just some dishes, an old tin basin, a prewar almanac, its corners nibbled by rodents, a few rusty utensils, no trace of recent use aside from the padlock on the front door chain open, not even forced. He takes advantage of this, still naked, to empty his backpack, the box of ammunition, the empty flask, the bandages, the blanket, he puts it all into the chest, takes the basin, the rifle, the flask, and goes out, fills the basin, plunges in his boots to wash the soles.

The sun beats down on his back, his chest, his legs,

here you're a little concealed by childhood,

hidden in childhood,
childhood manages to make you forget the war and hunger,
childhood lurks, it's a monster like any other,
you lie down on the heat of the big flat stone of the threshold.
He manages to close his eyes without imagining tortured faces
with bloody mouths and haggard eyes,
your body, after the water, after the sun, is losing its electrical
smell, of oil and blood, the smell that war has given it,
high up in the sky birds and planes are circling. They don't
see you. Could he reach them with the rifle? He'll have to hunt
for his food. A pigeon, a rabbit, a hare, which he can cook in the
fireplace. As a child, he was a patient hunter. Lying on his back in
the daylight, his eyes on the sky, he sees again the long hunting
parties in the fall: his father carried a measly blunderbuss with a
single barrel, vestige, relic that made a demonic racket—war has
made weapons proliferate, has sown and cultivated them, all kinds
of weapons, with their own specific names, rifles, guns, pistols,
revolvers, machine guns, cannons, mortars, shells, war is a change
in the number of things, names that appear, a sudden vibration
in the air, a steel bottle brush, a phial of mineral oil, a pain a loss
a fear an involuntary contact with the world of the projectile and
the wound, the fluid world of pain, exile and loss, the colorless
world of khaki, brown, and gray, the sage world of sweat, terror,
and screams. His hands are all full of corns and calluses, traces
of the wooden handle and the metal barrel, he suddenly gets up,
crouches down, he heard a noise, several abrupt noises, crackling
nearby, footsteps, he snatches up his weapon,
someone's coming, you can distinctly hear footsteps on the
other side of the garden wall, many footsteps that pause, silence
fixes everything in place, the footsteps must have seen your things
near the well, from afar,
someone's coming, or else the footsteps heard your naked heart
pounding, move the breech silently, remove the safety,
someone's coming, you can hear them stamping their feet,
many feet are beating the ground past the wall,

someone came, someone you can't hear anymore, you've hidden yourself crouching low near the porch behind the wall,

his left hand well-placed on the cross under the barrel, he is ready, he stands up all of a sudden, finger on the trigger, points the rifle at the other side of the wall, toward the olive trees and the orange tree, it's a woman, she's standing next to a mule or a donkey whose lead she's holding, she's wearing a long gray skirt, he doesn't shoot, she's wearing a bandanna tied at the bottom of her forehead like a peasant, he doesn't shoot, she's wearing a blouse with puffed sleeves, a black cardigan, there is horror on her face and her mouth wide open,

shoot, you're afraid as well, kill her get rid of her,

he doesn't shoot, the wall hides the lower part of his body, his nudity, he makes a movement with the barrel, without saying anything, upwards, a movement that has no meaning, a sign of the rifle,

shoot, kill her, get rid of the intruder violating your solitude,

he doesn't shoot, she tries to guess the meaning of the movement of the barrel like an unknown language, she suddenly raises her arms in the air, her face lengthened with fear—the donkey shakes its head and snorts, she doesn't let go of the lead.

He stands there dumbfounded, a muscle in the woman's pale cheek is trembling, her eyes seem to be misting over with tears. He recognizes terror on her face,

that way, go,

he guides her with the barrel of the rifle, she walks to the big threshold stone, he signals to her to continue to the cabin's wall, the donkey follows her even though she has let go of the bridle, she's facing the wall, her arms in the air stretched to the sky,

this is the moment, shoot,

he presses the trigger, the shot explodes, resounds against the rocks, echoes among the hills, the woman twists on herself, collapses, falls as if sitting in a strange position, chin collapsed on her chest, one arm half-raised, elbow folded against the stone wall.

The donkey starts braying, backing toward the olives and thickets.

He feels the heat of the barrel against his bare chest; he puts down the weapon, picks up his clothing spread out near the well, gets dressed, the smell stings him again, the war is back, on him, in him, all around him.

VI

On the Havel a little over twenty years ago, when Maja was still of this world, body, gaze, and soul, those three objects of Paul's passion. She confided in me, in the midst of her endless elucubrations between Spandau and Wannsee, how happy she was that the twentieth century was over; how happy she was to see Europe progressing and how ardently she wished the twenty-first century would never experience the horrors of the preceding century; she forgot she was talking to her daughter, I felt; she was addressing the historian—or an imaginary audience, listening to an impossible future political discourse. I had seen them all my childhood, Maja and Paul, all my life, running after each other from one side of the Iron Curtain to the other, from one side of the Berlin Wall to the other, from one side of imperialism to the other; I had seen them together and separately, the politician and the mathematician, he a famous and feted public personage from East Germany, a fervent Communist to the point of folly, and she, a politically active woman from the West, always suspected of spying for the enemy and I remember, in 1974, during the affair of the spy Günter Guillaume and the resignation of Willy Brandt, I remember how all eyes were trained on Maja, so much so that she'd had to put a hiatus on public appearances during the endless investigation—she didn't see either the GDR or of course Paul between 1974 and 1978, four long years of intense epistolary exchange, and even though, ever since 1972, it was much easier to go to East Berlin for residents of the West, Maja had withdrawn to Bonn and Göttingen, in a kind of desert crossing: I was twenty-one, I was visiting Paul once a week, on Elsa-Brändström-Strasse; I would ritually greet the bas-relief of the elephant over the front door, would climb to the second floor, the staircase smelled of East Berlin, that indescribable (and unforgettable) mixture of varnish, wood, cabbage, and coal. We'd eat lunch at his place or at Koch, the little restaurant on the Brunnenstrasse, and he'd walk me to the Friedrichstrasse train station before taking his streetcar back to Pankow: that was our Sunday outing. For me, it signified above all, morning and evening, hours of waiting in the rigmarole of customs between the station platforms—hours of tension on the way there, would they let me pass, hours of tension on the way back, would they let me leave? I'd arrive in the West exhausted, but every time I'd religiously call Maja from Steglitz to tell her the news.

Paul feared nothing and no one. He was a privileged person. He was a member of the Party; ever since 1967, he owned a passport from the German Democratic Republic, a permanent exit visa to go wherever he liked, and he almost never used it, aside from visiting Maja in the Federal Republic from time to time, very rarely. I remember the two conferences they went to in the West, Paris and Oxford (not counting Moscow, Prague, Budapest, and others) in his forty-year career. His terrain, his territory, was not travel in the way we understand it: if he was sometimes sad in Pankow, it was not, like most of his fellow-citizens, because he couldn't leave it. If he was sometimes sad in Pankow, it was because Maja wasn't there.

During dinner on the evening of Monday, September 10, 2001, at the White Owl inn in Wannsee, Robert Kant mentioned that very trip Paul took to Oxford in the mid-1970s; everyone was astonished, Kant said, laughing, that the East German government let him leave the country. Of course Paul's English colleagues were aware of Paul's political commitment, and his decision to remain in the GDR come hell or high water, Kant said, smiling. I remember how a dean in the division of sciences immediately offered him a teaching post as if he were some kind of refugee, fresh off the boat: Paul felt extremely humiliated, he even got angry and almost up and left without giving his series of lectures, Kant tittered. Half the campus was on the far left, at the time. Paul made a big impression with the students. They all already knew passages from *The*

Buchenwald Conjectures by heart—imagine their emotion when Paul launched into a kind of anti-Imperialist internationalist rant! The Vice Chancellor had turned red, but with rage.

Linden Pawley was sitting next to Robert Kant; I can see him again slicing his cutlet and agreeing to what Robert was saying—we too had wanted to invite him to Columbia, in the late 1980s. Pawley shook his head in disappointment. He always refused to come. Even after the reunification of Germany. Impossible. It's incredible, but he had no wish whatsoever to go to Columbia or to discover New York, Pawley added as he waved the schnitzel on the tip of his fork back and forth just as he shook his head before.

Maja smiled. She was familiar with Paul's intransigence. Jürgen Thiele was too.

"It was inconceivable, for Paul, to have 'normal relations' with Imperialism," Thiele added. "That was an obstacle to the Institute's development after 1991."

Maja of course took up the thread. She was on her own turf.

"Paul defined himself as 'an antifascist mathematician.' He was as stubborn as an axiom."

I remember smiling internally at this summary of my father's personality, *stubborn as an axiom,* Maja always had a gift for propaganda, sorry, for publicity—in my memory, in my childhood memories of Elsa-Brändström-Strasse, Paul wasn't quite so stubborn, not so politically blinded, quite the contrary, he inveighed against anything and everything; I remember him, after 1961, inveighing against isolation, the Wall, that ridiculous Wall, he said: sharing Paul's daily life didn't give the impression of sharing the existence of a staunch Marxist, or a Stalinist, or a devotee of Khrushchev, Brezhnev, or Honecker. I remember the long evenings among friends on the Elsa-Brändström-Strasse, before I was firmly sent off to bed, at around nine o'clock; they'd say a lot of bad things about the regime, the government, the institutions. Similarly, when we went to the movies, at the Colosseum on the Grimmstrasse, at the Tivoli on the Berliner Strasse, or elsewhere, on the way back, still on foot, never on the streetcar, Paul, usually in the middle of the street and without attempting to hide himself, used to vilify what he called "the intellectual rigidity of this country," most of whose writers, intellectuals and scholars he hated, it must be said, aside from his friends—for if he was stubborn in one thing, and perhaps this is what Maja had in mind when she asserted that *Paul was as stubborn as an axiom*, it was in friendship. My father, Paul Heudeber, was obstinate in friendship and in love. Fatally obstinate. His friends and lovers were much more infallible than the Party. His friends and lovers were never wrong: he would defend them, in private or public, come hell or high water. He would fight for them. He was even ready to compromise himself for them. For Maja or me, it goes without saying. For all of us.

The most difficult thing for Paul was when two of his friends, two of his comrades, argued violently and he had to side with one against the other. This violence of choice, of decision, would torture him to the point of paralysis: he would remain prostrate, shut away, pondering or fretting and sighing, for five minutes or five days, however long the altercation lasted. If an argument in Paul's living room became turbulent, you could be sure he'd suddenly disappear to go look for something urgently in the kitchen or lock himself up in the bathroom. If two people he liked equally squabbled, even in a friendly way, it would be torture for him. He had to wait for the tension to die down before he took sides—when there was no longer a side to take.

From that dinner, at the White Owl inn in Wannsee facing Peacock Island on September 10, 2001, two images have lingered:

— Maja's earrings, teardrop-shaped pendants, sparkle. The candle's yellow flame flickers in its holder. The tablecloth is red and white. Maja's hair is the color of the candlestick, pewter-gray. The gray pewter contrasts with the strawberry-red lipstick Maja overdid.

— Linden Pawley furtively looks at Maja, with great tenderness. I can sense a kind of veneration in that gaze, a submissive veneration I hadn't known he felt. As soon as he senses he is being observed, he turns away from Maja and stares into the distance, at a painting on the restaurant wall.

Prof. Dr. Paul Heudeber
Elsa-Brändström-Str. 32
1100 Berlin Pankow
GDR

Maja Scharnhorst

Sunday, February 5, 1961

It's 10 a.m. and it's snowing, my love. It seems as if the sun will never rise, never. Irina is still sleeping, I don't have the heart to wake her—do you remember those freezing dawns in Berlin that last a whole day, when the light wavers at the whim of clouds? It's been a month now since I've seen you and life is frozen in place. The things I've been thinking of are not very cheerful—the dates make it so. Twenty years. Twenty years ago I was locked up. In the camp among the beech trees. Today I'm over forty, Irina will turn ten this year. I feel as if I'm the same as I was at twenty, though. I haven't solved anything. I haven't made much progress. The question of the distribution of prime numbers that fascinated me at the time still haunts me. There should be a way to describe it simply. My demonstration of the infinity of twin primes was a first step. I have to move forward with new tools. Perhaps more topological than algebraic. I'm not getting at anything really new by exploring skew fields. Seen from our present knowledge, the distribution of prime numbers has all the appearance of chance. How is that? Far away, among the very large numbers suddenly appear galaxies of primes, regrouped, impossible to predict. As if we were always faced with the consequence of a hidden theorem.

Khrushchev wants to take the shrapnel, the debris, out of the heart of Europe, he says. West Berlin is a nail in his shoe. I prefer to think with pride that Socialism demonstrates every day the strength of that heart, the power of that Europe, and that it will soon be the puddle of capitalism that is West Berlin that will dry up on its own: the refugee camps won't be in Marienfelde anymore but in Köpenick, the inhabitants will beg us to receive them—which we'll do with open arms.

Twenty years ago, there on the Ettersberg hill, I was looking for absent stars and thinking about polynomial rings, prime numbers, all the misery around me, the pain that was increasing, illness, torture, and hunger, but mostly about you whom I had lost but whose face so often appeared to me: your face rose up to protect me. You protected my days as you protect them today, you even soften them in absence and Irina projects something of you, a softness, a consolation for the passage of time, a ray of light that comes from your close and distant soul. You are a malady—my passion has the malady of infinity, my love can only be written with your name. There is no other way to designate love but to say your name. Come back to me soon.

Paul

VII

She woke from her faint, regained consciousness, she's bleeding from her belly, she's wounded, she feels no pain, none whatsoever. She doesn't see the shirtless man who shot at her,

I'm going to throw up, my heart is about to explode,

she puts her hand under her skirt,

it's not blood, it's something else,

she gets her breath back. She looks for the donkey but doesn't see it. She gets up, almost collapses again, she really thought she was dying, everything turned black when the gun fired, everything got dark, where is the man, she's hesitant to run away, she's afraid he'll catch her, why did he spare her, the sun is burning, she goes back to the garden and the shade of the olive trees. The donkey is grazing on a thornbush, she strokes its neck, her eyes are full of tears, the perfume of leaves is wafting through the air, a scent of artemisia and warm animal. She wonders where to go, where to flee, she can't go back down to the village, she can't cross the wild mountains to the plain, she can't follow the summits to the north and to the border,

she is alone,

there he is again, standing up, right there on the flagstone, he's not carrying a weapon anymore, she looks at him, he says nothing, he has a beard, he has put on a stained military jacket, she can't guess his age, he has dark eyes with dark bags, she thinks she recognizes him, she lowers her eyes, why did he spare her, he has no idea, he watches her and wonders why at the last instant he lifted the weapon skywards, wasted a cartridge, maybe alerted a shepherd—but who's surprised by gunshots during a war, who,

you can't let her go, she knows you're here at the cabin, she knows who you are, does she know who you are, fear is on her face but who wouldn't be afraid, suddenly she recognizes him and her terror grows, he is the son of the ironmonger—and the thought is stifled in her brain, reaching neither language nor image,

evil is everywhere.

He observes her; he recognizes the face, even deformed as it is by fear, the scarf on her head, she should take it off, take it off he shouts, she takes it off and her too-short hair greasy from the cloth rounds out her face and makes it look terrifying, darker too, she puts the scarf away in one of the bags in the donkey's packsaddle,

a donkey like long ago, you haven't seen any animals including horses or mules since you were a child, what is there in this cargo,

he should have killed her, he should have killed this woman with a skull like a mangy monkey's, this woman with the skull of a man or a nun, but a great weariness seized him at the idea of the corpse, the remains, the blood, the grave to be dug, a laziness, and so now life is even more cumbersome than dead flesh. He stands there facing her without knowing what to say, he motions her over. She moves toward the porch, pulling the donkey. He takes the animal's lead, their fingers touch for a fraction of a second, she withdraws her hand as if his skin were burning. He ties the donkey to a big nail stuck high up in one of the wooden braces—they used to hang tobacco leaves from it to dry them—she shudders but obeys when he invites her into the shack, he doesn't follow her, he locks the door behind her with the padlock, there's no handle inside. Like trapping a fly under a glass, she'll walk round and round before sitting down and waiting. He briefly goes through the bags on the donkey's packsaddle, clothes smelling of laundry soap, personal objects, long needles like ones used for knitting, charms, photographs, souvenirs, thick round cakes wrapped in cloth, he eats one, they're shortbread biscuits filled with a sweet paste, baked goods for a fair, he eats another, he's a little ashamed, the way a child plunders a forbidden cupboard,

war has returned you to the savagery and solitude of childhood,

he puts the cakes back in the package, she was planning to leave for a long time, she was ready for exile, he takes a block of very dark, poorly cut green soap. He frees the donkey from its saddle, takes down the heavy bags, strokes the animal for a long time, on its endless neck, between its ears, the donkey rubs against him, its fur is silky, it smells of sweat and hide,

it's been a long time since you stroked an animal, so long since you've stroked one,

with the donkey and the rifle he could try to reach the border, he'd have to go back up into the mountain and follow the summits to the Black Rock then go back down almost to the sea, hide, conceal himself in the very belly of the war, in the folds of its bloody trenches, he suddenly realizes the donkey is one-eyed, its right eye is blue and white like a glazed marble, half-covered by its eyelid, its back bears wounds that are suppurating, he might have to kill it,

you don't know how to do anything but kill, you don't know anything about donkeys or animals, they have the innocence of their bestiality, not you, you wrap yourself in brutality like a cloak,

you've locked the woman up but she hasn't disappeared.

The air turns tense, clouds are piling up in the foothills, tar over indigo, ocher under cotton, the wind picks up a little, his clothes finished drying on his skin, he is hungry, he could devour the pastries carefully wrapped in their cloth, break the dry shells of almonds or devour oranges and lemons but he wants to hunt, the cartridge shot into the air woke a desire for game, for shooting, for a result. For solitude on the mountain.

He maneuvers the bolt on the cabin door, the woman is sitting motionless on the bench in the half light, he sets down his kit inside, gets his bag, closes the door behind him—he moves the donkey somewhere new, ties it to a tree near a bush that the animal immediately starts nibbling. He walks toward the summit, to the mountain pass he crossed the night before, he'll veer off to the east, toward a big area of scrub a little lower down, maybe a pheasant will emerge from its bushes, or a bustard, or a rabbit he'll skin with pleasure before quartering it and roasting it on the grill, ribs and haunches broken, flattened with a stone, the way his father used to do. He walks for an hour, then two, the clouds protect him from the sun, they're not harbingers of anything good, he's familiar with them, they'll gather together then become a thick fog that will drown the pass, engulf it in freezing cotton wool, then the first lightning bolt will tear through the mountain, a warmth will crack the cold, fat wet drops will stir up a smell of earth and then the rain will come, will roll the pebbles and fill the streams to the foam-muddled sea.

He keeps walking,

Lord soon it will be Good Friday,

you are ashamed when you think about His Name—the rifle leaning on you, you are walking through nature, His Nature,

everything is singing His praises and is adorning His glory,

he passes through the bushes, listens to wings beating, branches shifting. The shrubland is sheltered by two rocky slopes, in its center snakes a little dried-up stream; he climbs this narrow valley until he finds a perfect hideout, a rock sheltered from the wind, leaning against the slope, slightly overhanging the thickets of low shrubs (myrtle, heather, rockrose with yellow flowers, creased as if made of paper, balls of vegetation veined with brambles), which are invading what used to be the streambed. He lies down on the ground, his body hidden by the rock, rifle by his side; once again he's sorry he doesn't have binoculars anymore, a good pair of binoculars with which he could spot, without being seen, the slightest movement in the thickets. The sun is invisible behind the clouds, there are no shadows, no possibility of being dazzled by the light, animals come out to find a male or a female, to reproduce, build a nest, trim a burrow with grass, take part in the funereal passion of nature, funereal because there is always a rifle, a hawk, a predator ready to bloody this ballet with a claw, a talon, or a bullet. He breathes in deeply the perfume of hyacinth, gets drunk on thyme as he waits,

your memories are thrashing in a cage in the distance, you can live without them for a few hours,

he knows he'll put off the instant of firing as long as possible to take advantage of this rustling calm that seems more agitated the more you watch.

Sitting in the cabin in the dim light back very straight hands on her knees she waits for the moment of her rape, she waits horrified for the instant of her rape, she choked with fear when the man opened the cabin door, when his silhouette loomed against the light, she tensed all her muscles, clenched her teeth, she knows who he is, everyone knows who he is, he delayed her execution only to rape her before killing her,

the way a butcher keeps an animal in the pen alive so he can sacrifice it later,

the hut is quiet, she sometimes hears the cry of a bird outside; the beams and laths creak as they warm up, a lost fly spirals in the shadows, while the sun outlines a liquid beam of light on the threshold and the smell of ashes,

I could run away,

you just have to slip an object (cardboard, blade) between the door and the frame to lift the outside latch, there might be a chain she hasn't seen, a padlock she didn't hear open when he came in, and especially there's the man, how can she guess his position, she can no longer see his shadow inscribed in rays of night under the door. Maybe he left, with the donkey, and this possibility fills her with sorrow, the donkey is old and one-eyed but it's been close to her for so long, she dressed its wounds in its shelter, brought its hay, examined its feet, the donkey took care of her as she took care of it, where is it now, it's madness an immense risk she wants to find out the truth, she wants to reassure her heart, her heart, the one that's beating, she wants this, she gets up, snatches a metal bar near the ash bucket, slips the tip between the door and the wall, lifts it to raise the latch, she succeeds after several attempts, the door opens onto an overcast sky, almost black near the sea, she stands there unsure, poker in hand, there's no one outside, the donkey's saddle is there under the porch, there's no one, there's no one by the well, no one by the lemon tree, no one by the orange tree, she walks slowly forward, crosses the little wall, reaches the pebble-strewn field planted with olive trees, the man isn't there, the donkey is eating an acacia, reassured she walks over to it, it shoves its muzzle and forehead under her armpit to greet her and licks her hand, she pats its neck,

it's me, it's me, pretty animal,

the wounds on your back are oozing and not scabbing over,

I should take care of them before the flies get to them,

will the man reappear,

she knows who he is, this hut belonged to his father or his uncle,

God what will become of me,

she could take the bare necessities and run away with the donkey, toward the pass, the summits, not stay here waiting to be raped by that bladelike iciness,

Lord guide me and lead me to the right path, send me your sweet angels,

the pass, the summits, the border, the tears misting her eyes, this isn't a trip for a woman alone, no doubt she'll come across other fugitives, other exiles, a family, who knows, she could accompany them, let them make use of the donkey to carry their children,

the war has reset everything to zero, erased everything flattened everything filed everything down, automobiles charred by the roadsides the airplanes stains against the setting sun a throbbing sound a whistle and everything catches fire in screams of defeat, neighbors suddenly spit in front of you, their children take on airs and make threats, you become prey, you had been the masters you become prey for their dirty eyes, the war sullies children's gazes with hatred, hatred and weariness, everything increases, everything multiplies Evil and pain, the burn of rape is written across each sullied forehead, heads bow under the shame of shaved skulls, heads bow to be beaten.

She strokes the donkey and hugs its neck in her arms, it's all that remains from before the war, the donkey licks the sweat on her face, pale between the gleaming wings of her amber hair,

come on donkey, let's go, let's take the road to the pass, before that I'll give you something to drink, I won't put that idiotic pack-saddle back on, it's scraping you, let's go before the man gets back,

she pulls the donkey by the rope to the well, raises the metal lid and fills the tin pitcher the man left there, she splashes herself with freezing water, washes under her skirt while she lifts it, she's afraid of getting completely undressed, a brief wash then she waters the donkey who drinks greedily.

Dense white clouds hide the sun, a warm breeze reaches her from the distant sea, the solemn purple streak under the cotton sky.

She goes back into the house for a moment to get a few things, cloth, provisions, she rolls everything into two sheets that she knots, balances them on the donkey's withers—she lets the donkey take another long drink, despite her immense fear of the man coming back, the ogre coming back and finding his pantry empty of woman, she's heard about this man, he's worse than an ogre, she pulls the donkey to the opening in the wall, picks a few oranges from the tree, and starts climbing the path leading to the pass, the donkey behind her, wondering where she found the courage to escape this way—the man might have left by this same path, she's afraid of meeting up with him, what would he do, he'd surely hit her, take her back to the cabin, why did he lock her up otherwise?

to frighten me before he rapes me,

he'll pursue me, I don't know where to go, into exile, how to go into exile alone,

she walks quickly, the donkey behind her, climbs the slope that leads to the pass not knowing the man took this same path an hour earlier,

he lets wild thoughts go by, memories and wind,

your mind is white like the sky,

he waits behind the rifle, waits for a target, a movement in the foliage, it's a matter of patience, chance and patience, he can stay there till evening, till nightfall, in a few hours, if he moves the thoughts will flood in again, he smells the perfume of spring on the mountain, earth warmed by sun that morning before the sky was veiled in a lifeless shroud, up to now only two lizards have appeared in front of him, two lizards and a swarm of insects, he hears birdsong, sometimes the clack of their wings but no bird has ventured into his sights, the cartridge is in place, the trigger is very obedient, he is prepared, curiously the hunger has disappeared and given way to the excitement of the hunt,

don't let the thoughts come back, the woman, women, the woman you left sitting in the house, hands on her knees she was afraid of you, she gave off something you know well, her face, her shoulders, her body was full of terror, invisible spiders were climbing up her chest, you noticed those shivers, that smell,

he chases away that thought, erases it, watches a caper bush whose smooth leaves fall in branches against a flowering broom mingling the most disturbing green with the insolent yellow, the air is saturated with warm smells, powdered sun all around him— he moves, he shifts to stretch his arms and legs a little, he breathes, he has something like a tear in his eye come straight from child-hood, despair, hope, he doesn't know, a wild feeling that suddenly flees away, the sun tears through the clouds as if through the breast of a lamb, a luminous puddle stretches out between the spots of the shrubs, a luminous puddle stretches out over the rocks, the pebbles, so many reefs on a dazzled sea, strewn with green islets, something trembles, he smells, feels the proximity of the shot, something trembles in the light, something is going to appear, something is going to rustle, the sun will set everything in motion, it's a bird flying up, a fat red fowl with gray stripes, a partridge, he just has to lift the barrel of his rifle a little to follow it, he shoots, he holds the weapon against his shoulder with his left arm, the noise is abrupt and powerful, his eye is still fixed on the bird, he thinks he can see a spray of blood and feathers, before the distant fall into the little valley, the burning cartridge case hits the ground with the sound of glass, the air smells of war now, the acrid odor of the explosion, he waits, partridges often travel in flocks, he has taken note of the spot where the creature fell, over there, near that cactus, he waits, lying between the stones. No other bird,

you'd do better to go and get the quarry before you lose sight of the spot,

he slips on the gun strap, the metal is warm against his back, he thanks the Lord for this catch, goes down the dry valley, there on a cracked white limestone mound a cluster of cacti is growing, devil's tongues, green and prickly, the partridge fell there, it is impaled on a fat spiny leaf dripping with vermilion blood, its neck is ripped out, none of the crop is left. He picks it up by the feet. He gathers a dead branch, ties the bird to the stick with a bramble, carries his prey on his left shoulder, a bloody bundle, he climbs up a little between the rocks and the thickets of heather—the flowering rosemary is buzzing and just like the pistachio trees exhaling its medicinal perfume, its pharmaceutical smell so surprising in nature,

you've gone only once to the infirmary, not for no reason as they believed, you had no wound, but it was not for nothing, a great invisible pain you didn't explain,

nature itself calls war to mind,

nature,

again he lies down in wait, he still has many shots left in the magazine, enough for all the partridges on the mountain, all the wood pigeons and all the hares.

VIII

On September 10, 2001, at the White Owl inn in Wannsee, across from the island with the peacocks and the riverboat *Beethoven*, during dinner, the day before the opening of the "Paul Heudeber Days," we talked much more about the Heudeber legend, the Heudeber statue, than about my father. That's logical: Pawley and Kant were among those who had contributed most to erecting it, that statue: Pawley, Kant, and Maja, who, if I am to believe this extract of my journal at the time, written in my cabin after we went back on board the *Beethoven* as its mooring lines were gently agitating the dark waters of the lake, were slightly drunk as they left the restaurant:

Dinner Jürgen Thiele—Linden Pawley—Robert Kant—Maja. White Owl inn at Wannsee. Candles. Everyone drank a lot. Mixture of great joy and profound sadness at the mention of Papa. Pawley was stammering, alcohol or emotion or both. Maja made me a little ashamed, drinking and flirting, at her age. Fear (or deep desire) that this whole little crowd might accidentally fall into the lake as they walk back to the boat.

What an awful impression, rereading oneself after twenty years have elapsed. Much worse than finding an old photograph. I can remember taking the air afterwards on the boat's deck before going over the talk I'd give the next morning, putting in order my transparencies for the paper I would give to open the conference, a paper entitled "Mathematics and Resistance." The next entry in my journal (written probably after breakfast) is no less salty:

Got up at dawn—pain in the abdomen. Typical for days of stage fright. Opened the curtains to the sun illuminating the castle on Peacock Island, over there beyond the trees, on the other side of the river. So beautiful you could cry—another effect of all the emotion. Thought about Papa. How not to disappoint him. Who, here, is going to be interested in Nasir al-Din Tusi, in mathematics at the time of the Mongol invasions? In that old Shiite, that recluse in the mountains of the Assassins? In his vision of irrational numbers? In his circles, his ellipses, his orbits? What solitude.

The solitude of that historian of mathematics, read by neither historians, nor mathematicians.

The solitude of the historian of mathematics, then, on the verge of old age, in her Berlin apartment on Schlossstrasse in Steglitz, the noisiest street in the neighborhood, an apartment located above the one my mother rented until 2005.

Maja Scharnhorst was an abandoned child, who had been given the family name of an old Prussian general, God knows why—legend has it that she was found, one morning at dawn, at the foot of the statue of said general in Berlin, next to the Neue Wache, on Unter den Linden. My recent research into the archives of the time confirm merely that the child was entrusted to the orphanage with a note mentioning her name, "Maja Scharnhorst," with no details of the circumstances of her discovery, her birth, or even her date of birth, which was decided by guessing the infant's approximate age. (Many of Maja's friends, enemies and colleagues thought she was one of the descendants of the abovementioned general, and that her actual name was Maja *von* Scharnhorst, but that she didn't use the particle out of political conviction—she never did anything to disabuse them.) Maja was an orphan of the Revolution, then a child of the Weimar Republic, raised in the "Lindenhof" orphanage in Lichtenberg, an orphanage founded by the pedagogue Karl Wilker. Unlike most orphans, simply raised at the time like farm animals in order to become submissive wives and efficient mothers, she had access to an education, then even found money to pursue her studies; she went to a girls' secondary school in which, as she herself says in her memoirs, she learned much less than in the local branch of the Socialist Party, which went underground after July 1933. When she was fifteen, the Party was already starting to use her to carry messages, to link together the comrades spread across the four corners of immense Berlin: who would be suspicious of a girl? No one mistrusted her. Not even in the League of German Girls, a Hitler youth organization to which she belonged under duress until she left Germany in 1938.

Maja was a figure of the Resistance and of Democracy.

Maja abandoned me for her political career just as she herself had been abandoned.

For a long time I felt an anger toward her that verged on silent hatred.

Dr. Paul Heudeber
Elsa-Brändström-Str. 32
1100 Berlin Pankow
GDR

Maja Scharnhorst
Pankow, 30 August 1961

My love,

Reality of isolation: we have built a barricade against fascism. In concrete and in one night. Or almost. We are now great and invincible—of course the West is surrounded and conquered. Everything depends on how all of this is considered; the principle of infinity is that there is always a greater quantity to imagine. Everyone was peacefully at the beach when a wind of panic rolled up their towels and sent their parasols flying, launching the flurry of return to Berlin and the endless lines (!!!) to get onto the S-Bahn with weapons and luggage and go to the West before (seemingly) all movement would be forbidden. I saw an avalanche of vacationers suddenly returning to work, who had "come back ahead of time." No one understands anything, apparently the decision was made at the highest level and in the greatest secrecy. (This "greatest secrecy" was relative since part of the Institute's personnel went to the West just before the fateful Sunday, thereby demonstrating that *the greatest secrets* are so only for the soldiers among them.) We now officially consider West Berlin as a loop in a plane, as in the topology of Poincaré: that is, of no real importance. In a game of Go, West Berlin would have disappeared and been replaced with white beads, our white beads. Apparently the Party is regarding this move as necessary and urgent. I confess it very selfishly annoys me because *our* movements will become more complicated, it seems. We don't know if these measures against terrorism, fascism, and capital are temporary or definitive. By chance I found out that since neither you nor Irina reside in the former Soviet-occupied zone but in the American sector, you don't run the risk of being held here against your will, if you ever feel like coming to visit me, which I do not advise for now. I hope our governing authorities will have a change of heart and will soon return to the edification of communism instead of getting lost in the intricacies of barbed wire. Comrades are not animals to be penned in ... They've forgotten that twenty years ago we were in other camps ... locked up in just the same way. Always the question of surfaces: I wonder if I am on side A or side B. Is it Reinickendorf that's suddenly behind a wall or Treptow?

Still, I'll put up with a wall between you and me if it helps the Socialist cause. I acknowledge that's a contradiction, but contradictions, when they are not made in bad faith, are the visible parts of great theorems that are yet to be formulated.

Is your vacation going well? Is Irina finally swimming? (Please don't tell her I asked that question!) In early July, at the lake, she didn't want to get in past her waist, despite the encouragements of other children. It should be said that there were ducks, and swimming in ducks ... would have disgusted me too.

Write soon, or go to the post office and call me at the Institute, fascism hasn't yet cut off the telephone,

I miss you,

Paul

IX

She heard the gunshot, the echo rolled between the slopes, she stood still on the path, the donkey came closer to her,

that could be him, he's not far away, he'll kill me this time, if I meet him he'll kill me,

she hesitates, tries to determine where the vanished sound had originated, the disappearing echo, why would he kill her, if he didn't do it the first time, he'll keep her like flesh for rape, she understands, she's heard the women talking in the village, whispering, murmuring without moving their lips, amongst themselves, tears in the corners of their eyes, eyelids squeezed together in rage and shame, she also heard the man's first name and his family name, they had recognized him, the men, the women, defiled, wounded, broken or dead, it was him, he was one of them, over there, his friends and him, him and his cousins, the brutes, the torturers, the rapists, impossible to call them soldiers,

must walk to the north, to the border I know nothing about, the people, their language, their differences,

she returns to the pass, sees the clouds piling up their blackness in the foothills, the sea, all of a sudden, is invisible, hidden by an ominous gray line, a cotton army advancing. The donkey nudges her with its forehead to reassure her, she smiles at it, strokes it between the ears, she suddenly realizes that dozens of invisible birds are singing all around her, have they always been there, they fell silent at the gunshot, do they know what a gunshot is, they've started singing again,

every day the spring is rising a few meters up the mountain until it covers the ground with its veil, hides it under its canopy, the flowers are blooming, nests are growing, bees are bathing in the pistils, more and more of them, the scorpions are extricating themselves from their sticky eggs and the snakes are moving, in a rustle of impatience, an excitement of rutting,

she is not alone, she is with the donkey, she is with her memories: she knew that running away was impossible, that escaping meant the sea or death, she hasn't been spared the destruction that befell the village, over there in the hollow of the hills, she must climb the mountain at least to the ruins, to the Black Rock, and she'll be hidden, concealed, as she thought she could have been in the hut by the olive trees. In every age people have hidden in the ruins of the Black Rock, mystics and fugitives, that castle with no other guardian than the wind and the vultures, the Black Rock is near the border; maybe other refugees are stopping there, gathered around invisible fires in the hollow of the ruins, she has to pluck up her courage and hope. The memory of the man and his gun has become less burning, she walks toward the north,

I'll leave death and shame behind me,

shame and defilement,

I'm walking on the mountain with a donkey the way they did a hundred years ago, a thousand years ago, I have provisions, water in a can,

she regains her strength in the shreds of sunshine sweeping the rock-strewn ground.

The sun had long since passed through the gate of noon when he decided to go back to the cabin, three blood-soaked birds hanging from his stick, two woodpigeons and a partridge, the ringdoves blue and gray, the partridge red with dark stripes, he is happy as a child, happy with his shots, happy with the impending feast, happy to have rediscovered this mountain pleasure, sated with warmth, scents, and sounds,

you've managed not to worry either about yesterday or about tomorrow, you've managed to spend those hours without a thought in your head, without a pain,

blinded by the memory of your father, blinded by childhood that takes over everything,

you are a man without a tomorrow, condemned to yesterday and today,

he's not worried about the air raids screaming over the cities any more than he is about the black smoke that mingles suffering with the clouds, flinging powdered death into the sun, or about the cries of humans and animals, which are often the same, the same cries the same animal deaths,

the ones you pushed into mass graves are coming back to you, the ones who were lost even down to their names, covered over, entombed, weighed down with bullets in a cluster of life, blood, death,

he chases away this thought like the others while he watches the clouds darkening, the sky becoming dense: thunder rumbles, far away, near the sea where abrupt sparks briefly split the horizon, he'll be back at the hut before the storm reaches this far, if it does—once at the cabin he'll heat up a pot on a fire of branches, he'll gut the birds before plunging them into the boiling water and then, while the fire slowly dies out, he'll pluck them, cut them in half—finally he'll roast them and eat them burning hot, his hunger obsesses him, it accompanies him among the rocks and the dense thickets, the thorn bushes, the twisted black pines, the old abandoned olive trees, his hunger accompanies him in his descent to the shack, rifle on his right shoulder, bloody bundle on his left, he had forgotten the woman, he hopes she ran away, that she managed to lift the latch and run away, he doesn't want any more shivers of fear and pain,

you should have killed her, now she knows you're at the cabin, she recognized you, you read it on her face,

whatever the case, you can't stay here, hunt your food this way like a savage, Lord, have mercy, you'll have to set off again

tomorrow, when tomorrow comes you'll start off toward the north, then before the border you'll abandon the rifle and pass yourself off as one of the conquered, a loser, one of those the war has undone like badly tied knots,

suddenly he remembers his great youth,

this will be the beginning of something else you know nothing about.

He could perhaps wait one or two days before leaving, feed himself on the hunt and on fruit, take advantage of this time outside of the war, where the knife plunges only into the guts of birds, where you break the limbs of birds, where bullets go into birds—how much time will he need to reach the border, three, four days at most, he'll have to walk at night and hide out during the day, definitely, the further north you go, the more soldiers there are, deserters and bandits abound, a whole universe in flight, a whole world unraveled, the foam of evil flows from the mouth of the country, oozes between the teeth of victory. Since he left the hut, since he abandoned the vehicle without any gas, since he deserted the camp of conquerors, never before had he thought with so much precision about the meaning of his flight, the reality of his desertion,

you're nothing now but a spineless coward, a stench of solitude, the strength of soldiers comes from their numbers, the crowd, the camaraderie,

soldiers watch each other in rape and torture,

a deserter alone is good for nothing but the rope, the noose,

they won't waste any bullets on him,

they'll hang him from a branch by the roadside so everyone can see him, his jacket lowered to the middle of his biceps, hands tied behind his back, he'll swing slowly, children will throw stones that will scare away the crows eating his tongue, black outside of his mouth,

how many will there be, hanging by their necks by the side of the highway?

Suddenly right in the middle of the path he notices some equine shit, a pile of black and greenish lumps like kidneys streaked with straw, still fresh, there can't be many horses brought up to this pass, the woman must have fled with the donkey—why did she leave her village like that, alone, he didn't kill her, didn't rape her but others will, he hadn't thought of the journey of that woman, of her courage, she recognized him, but does he know her, does he want to remember these people, recall the humiliations, the bullying, the spitting,

you can't remember the woman's place in the brutality of childhood,

you don't want the vexations of the past to suffocate you,

the humiliations, you've tortured and massacred them,

he quickens his pace, hurries forward down the slope to the cabin and his refuge.

X

In Wannsee, on the morning of the start of the "Paul Heudeber Days," twenty-one years ago. We were waiting for fifty or so registered attendees, plus a few students who had come as observers from Potsdam or even Berlin, brave enough to bear the little hour-long walk (or a quarter of an hour by bicycle) that separated us from the nearest suburban train station. The riverboat's main salon—its main cabin, I should say—was full of black folding chairs; the iridescent light of the lake flooded the starboard side of the room through large square windows—on the other side, you could only see the concrete of the quay to which the *Beethoven* was moored.

Naturally the participants all sat on the light-filled side.

And so the room looked unbalanced, odd; I remember being very afraid the cabin would remain that way, half-empty, and that the boat, heeling too much to the lake side, would end up capsizing.

I had stage fright.

Maja kept pestering me about trivial things, Irina this, Irina that. Jürgen Thiele had set up a large whiteboard with sheets of semigloss paper and big black and red markers, metal cylinders whose smell—a mixture of chemicals and childhood—was reassuring, when you took off the cap.

I found the program in my files:

9 a.m.—Acknowledgements—Introductions
9:05 a.m.—Opening Speech
"Opening of the Paul Heudeber Days"
by Maja Scharnhorst
9:15 a.m.—First session: *Origins*

(1) "Mathematics and Resistance"
by Irina Heudeber
(2) "The First Ettersberg Conjecture,
Or, Mathematical Introspection"
by Robert Kant
(3) Discussion—Moderator: Linden S. Pawley
11 a.m.—Coffee break
11:30 a.m.—Second Session:
Analysis

My "mathematical" paper on the irrational numbers of Nasir al-Din Tusi was planned for the next morning, for the session devoted to number theory: the highlight of this morning was of course not Tusi at all, but a presentation of a recent development of Paul's theorem.

"Mathematics and Resistance" briefly discussed my father's life in the 1930s and '40s, and compared his fate with that of other European mathematicians, including Albert Lautman, executed in 1944 near Bordeaux for his part in the Resistance; Edmund Landau, whose classes at Göttingen Paul had attended, who died in 1938 in Berlin; Emmy Noether, who was his mentor in mathematics, forced into exile in 1933; the Polish mathematician Tadeusz Ważewski, interned at the Sachsenhausen concentration camp; and Felix Hausdorff, who committed suicide in January 1942 to escape deportation. It was primarily a brief homage to Paul Heudeber's antifascism; his youthful activity in informal communist networks that were struggling to survive in the university; his flight to Belgium with Maja; his detention in the Gurs camp in 1940; his arrest in Liège in 1941 and his deportation to Buchenwald, near Weimar, until the liberation of the camp on April 11, 1945, and his subsequent move to Berlin.

Maja's speech was of course very moving to me, moving and irritating, and so it was with slightly stinging eyes that I took my place in front of my mic, between Pawley and Robert Kant. Maja had sat down in the first row, and I thought that the moment must have been extremely moving for her too, even though she showed no emotion. I noticed that her right hand, which held the text of her speech, was trembling slightly.

It's hard for me to remember my feelings as I was giving my talk; and I can't seem to remember the discussion that Pawley led (brilliantly, without a doubt)—it's all buried beneath the ruins of the afternoon's collapse. A question from a student comes to mind about the demonstration (nonexistent at the time) of Paul's First Buchenwald Conjecture to which Pawley replied with a diagram and two formulae that were the only signs drawn on the whiteboard during the entire conference. When Jürgen dismantled it, before leaving the boat, he tore down this sheet, which he offered me as a souvenir, with his most apologetic air—I can see myself again throwing it away on the suburban train that took me back to Steglitz.

I dreamed of you this morning war is here
I dreamed of you all around me
Vibrating
A gentle explosion my heart of your presence
War is here this morning I dreamed of you
Perfect as the equations that send the shells flying
Perfect as the obviousness of the equations
Perfect as violence
Whole
You were there in me
I was alone
Everyone could talk of nothing but the war
I had nothing but you
And the sadness of your disappearance

Paul

[A note in a different hand, on the bottom, in pencil, Maja no
doubt: Liège, September 1, 1939]

XI

It began with the smell that rose up from the ground, the scent of
warm rock and slate, before the donkey started shivering, braying,
and walking too quickly; then the first drops, wet, fat, few, left
brown marks on the sandy earth of the path. The sun suddenly
disappeared; the light was purplish, strident, it was an interior light,
as if the evening had already fallen, the evening is already here,
she turned to look at the sky, pulled on the lead, tried to reassure
the donkey—the thunder crushes the earth with its exploding,
endless rage, cramped in the mountains, which it seems to split
apart; the thunder opens up the sunny side as it rolls, the infinite
thunder runs under the lightning flashes, jerky, abrupt sparkle of
giants splitting the rocks with its crackling—lightning hit close by,
lighting always hits very close, she can smell its scent of ozone, its
light has blinded the donkey's one eye with an awful reflection, the
drops of water have become trickles, straight streams, opaque curtains of continuous rain, an instant deluge whose force is starting
to shift the pebbles under her feet, the slope becomes a torrent in
the thunder that resumes and rumbles again, crushing any hope of
a refuge, she is immediately soaked, she is dripping, she looks for
a nonexistent shelter, the rain strikes the ground as strongly as the
thunder itself, she walks a few feet to the right, then returns to the
left at a run, stunned, the donkey bellows at each thunderclap, it
brays like a mad thing, adding its cries to the tumult, the lightning
flashes, the thunder doesn't stop, it's a repeating gun that makes the
earth shake, interspersed with huge electric arcs slicing through
the very mass of the rain. She notices the dark shadow of an oak
standing out in the storm, she runs toward the meager refuge, with
the donkey dragging its feet; everywhere torrents, waterfalls are
forming and hurtling down the mountainside: the whole flank of

the mountain collects the water and lets it flow toward the sea. The wind rises; between thunderclaps, it whirls, screaming, and redoubles its gusts until they're parallel to the ground, hurls waves of rain against bodies, as if the sea itself had invaded the mountain; the downpours stubbornly continue to beat the ground,

I'm soaked down to my bones, there's no recess, no rock hollow, nothing but this tree,

she reaches the trunk and leans against it, despite the storm the donkey eats the tough little green leaves on the lowest branches, she's afraid, the clouds are of a limitless black, she is dripping, her scarf, her short hair, her face are covered in tiny rivulets, the water is streaming down her shoulders, slipping between her breasts; her socks are swimming in the muddy torrents that span the tree roots and form miniature rapids, and when the storm is at its height, she thinks, as the darkened horizon is twisted with lightning flashes punctuated by rumblings, the madness of the rain seems to interrupt itself only to return twice as strong; it becomes thick, white, hard, and rebounds against the rocks, a stinging swarm of thousands of insects, the lower part of her legs, between her ankles and the hem of her skirt, is attacked by white hailstones that bounce back wherever they can, adding to the sonorous panic, to the infernal noise of the thunder, it's an army of millions of ice soldiers furiously stomping on the slopes, suddenly the air is freezing, as if smoking with frost—the donkey has started braying again, it's complaining about the hail, it's complaining about this painful mass on its back, it too is seeking the cover of the tree, whose dark branches, thin at the ends, are themselves victims of the hailstones and produce the muffled sound of a semantron struck by hordes of mallets, ice marbles are piling up against the rocks, in the crevices, on the slightest ledge, and are painting the landscape in a heavy, bluish, translucent snow which reflects the lightning and produces a morbid light, a sickly, fantastical phosphorescence.

At the instant when the downpour seems to be about to stop, when the sky's ammunition and the rhythm of the hailstones is slowing down, when the taste of fear and snow in her mouth gives way to that of broken flowers, grasses crushed by the storm's violence, when the wind itself seems to have exhausted itself from madness, when she lets herself relax and sigh and smile at the donkey, saying to it

you're soaked too, poor thing, we're sopping wet, I'm cold,

a huge explosion bursts, flings her and the donkey several meters away, in an enormous blast of wood, branches, splinters, flames, onto the wet ground, pursued by the insane light, by the smoking leaves growling over their heads, the sounds of crushing, of the destruction of all things whistling in her ears, the sudden smell of burnt wood, water vapor, and flint, the smell of the blazing sky, the smell of instantaneous fire, of immediate combustion in the crackling of the rocks, the roar of the detonation of lightning.

They both lie there, the woman and the donkey, three meters apart, it was neither a bomb, nor a shell, she'd never seen the power of lightning, she opens her eyes onto a tree burning, broken open and overrun with flames like shivers in which the rain, which has redoubled, is smoking. She feels pain rising up from her legs, her torso; the donkey has gotten up, it's swaying its head, as close as possible to the ground, lost, whining like a puppy, limping from one foot to the other, almost falling each time, from its mouth dark blood is dripping and splattering into blossoming flowers in the water on the rocks,

God, I beg Your forgiveness, is it really Your heaven that has just struck me, struck us, we deserve only war and fire, there is no strength, no power, except in God,

she is unable to stand up, she is overcome with an immense dizziness, she faints again, the rain covers her bloody hair with tears, her blackened cheeks, her broken shoulder, her milky thigh from which an obscene, smoking branch is sticking out, planted there like a spear.

XII

Among the stories that Paul told me to put me to sleep when I was little, almost every night, I would clamor for the tale of the Paris conference of the International Congress of Mathematicians in August 1900. Paul would sit down on the edge of my bed and would start by asking me:

"What story would you like me to tell you?"

And I would reply:

"The one about the Paris Conference!"

"So be it," Paul would say. His story always started with a description of the city: "Imagine the 1900 Paris Exposition," he'd say. "The whole world was there, on the banks of the Seine. Imagine the Seine, with its gilt bridges, its lion statues, the Seine flowing at the foot of the Eiffel Tower, imagine the Eiffel Tower, its millions of bolts as in a Meccano set, steel bolts and beams, imagine the bustling pavilions of dozens of nations from all over the world, imagine that the capital of the world wasn't Moscow yet," Paul would say. "The capital of the world was Paris," he'd say. "In one of the Exposition pavilions in Paris there was an astronomical telescope that was sixty meters long, powerful enough to count pedestrians on the moon. There was a terrestrial globe several dozen meters in diameter; there was the first rolling sidewalk in history, the first outdoor cinema with a giant screen. And it was there, in August, right in the midst of these wonders, that the greatest mathematicians on the planet had decided to meet, to discuss the latest advances and innovations in all the different domains of mathematics," said Paul. "They wore beautiful hats, tailcoats and long mustaches. The leader, the most brilliant of them all, the one who had opened up unknown spaces in algebra, was a Frenchman named Raymond Poincaré."

Point carré, square point! I couldn't believe his surname could be so closely linked to mathematics. "It's very common in France," Paul said. "In France, there are butchers named Monsieur Leboeuf"—and those words which I could understand in French, *carré, boeuf*, delighted me. A butcher named beef! A mathematician named square point! Then Paul would go on to the description of the conference itself:

"The scholars were thirsty," he'd say, "it was very warm that summer, when the most important mathematicians had gathered first in a magnificent café, the Café Voltaire, the day before the official opening of the Conference, to discuss the creation of the Secret Society of Analysts which would be forbidden to geometricians."

My childhood would rise up at each of Paul's attempts to transform his own story:

"No, that's not true! They gathered at the Café Voltaire to prepare their discussions for the next day!"

Paul would smile and end up agreeing. Then, for the *thousandth* time, he'd describe how Poincaré had been made President of the Conference, then he would point out who would chair each of the sessions, Moritz Cantor for history of mathematics (my favorite, of course), David Hilbert for analysis, and so on.

Why was the little girl that I was so passionate about these mathematicians in tailcoats, top hats, and mustaches, probably because they held a secret, the secret of my father's life, which I wanted to pierce, understand, unveil, explain. The Paris Congress opened the twentieth century up to scientific hope; the Paris Congress spelled out objectives for the part of humanity that was interested in mathematics, and in these scholars, my childhood saw saviors.

My father walked on two legs: algebra and communism. These two limbs allowed him to make his way through all of life. These two worlds allowed him to survive when he was deported. These two worlds grew, I imagined, from the Paris conference at the 1900 Exposition, from its top hats, Ferris wheel, and Metro. In the

wording of Hilbert's problems, which seemed to me — a strange
summary of Paul's magic — the logical consequence of the Worker's Second International of 1889: Paul's stories about mathematics and mathematicians were superimposed on what I was able to
learn about the history of Marxism-Leninism; the iron of the Eiffel
Tower reminded me of the strikes of the miners who had extracted
ore from the earth. For Paul, Paris was the symbol of the worker's
struggle and of colonialism: Göttingen represented knowledge
and mathematics and Berlin, Berlin was all of those things at once,
darkness tinted with hope. I remember asking him, in the 1980s,
when his life in the capital of East Germany seemed very weighty
and messy to me, Why did you settle in Berlin in 1945, why didn't
you go back to Göttingen? He replied that he had *won* Berlin in the
war, that it was booty captured from the Nazis, that the transformation of Berlin into a metropolis of utopia had to be completed. Four
years in the camp gave them, him and his comrades, the right to
take Berlin and try to lead the country toward communism. Toward
happiness. I never dared ask him if he still believed in that, but his
sadness in March 1990 with the results of the first free elections in
the GDR (the huge victory of the Right), then his astonishment at
the moment of the disappearance, pure and simple, of the Democratic Republic in the fall of that year, tend to show that the answer
was yes. In my father's last letters, the ones written just before his
death in the fall of 1995, there's a kind of sad detachment, a sudden
political apathy, a melancholy — starting in the late 1960s and his
voluntary "reclusion" in algebraic topology and utopian surfaces,
an imprisonment from which he wouldn't emerge until the early
1980s to take over the running of the Institute, one has the impression that melancholy is gaining ground, that he's starting to be
overwhelmed by it. Ten years of sadness — did this sadness have to
do with Maja, with the sensation of distance, almost of separation?
Those years I spent studying in Cairo, perfecting my Classical Arabic and learning the history of mathematics, Paul almost never
saw Maja. He met her in passing, now and then, according to their
letters: once in Hamburg, where Paul went for some official reason

or other, and once in Paris—another letter alludes to that. Maja believed that the Prague Spring (especially the position of the GDR on "socialism with a human face") had profoundly wounded Paul. Wounded, destroyed. "The Prague Affair" had tested his faith. He found no justification for the Soviet intervention—Walter Ulbricht's visit to Prague on August 12, eight days before the tanks entered Prague, eroded Paul's trust. For my father, all these events were so many blows against socialism. For Paul, the Soviets were more and more becoming enemies of actual socialism, as they had been during Stalin's time. Stalin did indeed conquer Nazism, but he had also imprisoned, deported, assassinated, purged Paul's heroes, all the revolutionaries of '17; Paul had also been outraged to learn, much later, that, after the liberation of Buchenwald, the Soviets had continued to use the camp to intern prisoners there, until as late as 1950. Nazi prisoners, true, but the fact that they could so simply "resume" the camp's operation, regard it just as a prison like any other, was, for Paul, quite simply an insult to the memory of all those who had died there. In the same way—and this is one of the few party decisions that my father openly criticized—the destruction of the concentration camp in 1950, with the exception of the crematorium and the bastions at the entrance, was to him a huge mistake. Buchenwald should have been not just a monument to the glory of antifascism, it also should have been a reminder of the sufferings of all those who were deported and tortured there. All those things were like tiny breaches: they never really undermined the solidity of the wall, Paul's communism.

Paul Heudeber bore the name of a little village in the mountains of the Harz District, from which his family probably came. Paul was born and lived with his parents until 1923 in the little town of Gernrode, before my grandfather Arthur, Paul, and his two sisters moved to Göttingen. My grandfather Arthur, a veteran of the First World War, had obtained, through some cousins, a job as a porter and factotum at the University of Göttingen; his wife Gertrud, my grandmother, had succumbed to an illness the year before. Göttingen was the city of mathematics, where Gauss and

Riemann taught, along with of course David Hilbert, until his retirement in 1930 (Paul recalls seeing him, impressively tall and with a Viking beard, having a discussion with Emmy Noether and the other teachers, one day when he accompanied Emmy to her office), David Hilbert and an immense list of scholars made Göttingen the capital of mathematics until 1933, when anti-Jewish laws, the great bloodletting of German scholarship, removed from the universities the most brilliant minds—including Emmy Noether, forced at the end of 1933 to exile herself to the United States.

Emmy Noether was more than a mother for Paul. She conceived affection for this child living on the ground floor of her apartment building, and he became so attached to her that at the age of seventeen he was her most brilliant student. The most brilliant and the most ignorant, said Paul. Paul was constantly singing Emmy Noether's praises; he talked about her all the time, so much that for me she is a kind of grandmother, or an aunt who died too young (she died in 1935) for us ever to have the chance to visit her (I'm sure that, had she lived, Paul would have agreed to go to the United States). A chapter from *The Buchenwald Conjectures* is devoted to her, the one about rings and ideals:

With Emmy
I was like those temple dogs
In India
Who they say know,
They learn from the masters and the Goddesses, though they cannot speak:
I was
Infused with science without understanding
The rings that Emmy placed on my fingers
The strings that she knotted in my hair.
Emmy Noether was tenderness,
All tenderness,
She caressed me with her mathematical hands
She drowned me with concepts and love
Love of equations and socialism

She took me on walks
Sat me down
Explained to me
Drew me
Embraced me with concepts, love, and socialism
With ideals—primary ideals in one ideal:
Intersection,
Rings:
Whole pairs form an ideal of the ring of wholes

My father had told me that he'd spent more time with Emmy than with anyone else in his childhood and adolescence—she made him work on problems of arithmetic and algebra all day; at the age of ten, he knew what a Diophantine equation was and knew the different types of solutions of $ax + by = c$ for natural numbers. Emmy never compelled him. She never forced him to do anything. In the morning, Paul would mount the steps leading to Emmy's apartment, four at a time, despite his sister's shouts, Leave the professor alone why don't you, he would have breakfast with her, a slice of bread pudding and a math problem, then he'd go back downstairs to get his schoolbag and run to school; when, a little later, my Aunt Ilse heard Emmy Noether coming downstairs to go to the Institute of Mathematics, she would open the apartment door a little and ask Emmy to please forgive Paul for his intrusion, to which Emmy would always reply, smiling, that she was very happy for his company, and that it was out of the question and that Paul should certainly come later for a snack too, since she had to correct his exercises.

In a documentary about women in mathematics filmed a few months before Paul's death, when he is asked what he learned from Emmy Noether, my father (burgundy wool vest, velvet jacket, white mustache), after rather a long pause, facing the camera, replies in the high, slightly timid voice of people who aren't used to being filmed: *Everything—but especially to be generous, to be interested in other people.* The journalist had been expecting a mathematical answer; she is obviously completely taken aback by Paul's reply, so she insists, And in mathematics? What did she teach you? Then Paul assumes his serious look, the serious look that with him often hides an ironic answer, which in this instance is not: *She taught me that mathematics was the other name for hope.*

XIII

The birds were already crackling on the embers when it started to rain. Fat, lazy drops spotted the rock. He salivates at the aroma of the meat, the scent of the fire; the fowl have become smaller now, plucked of their feathers, though a few resistant shafts stand out on the skin shriveling up as it browns—he gazes at them with desire, devours them in his imagination; the rain bounces off the metal lid of the well, streams in a thick curtain from the edge of the porch roof, the thunder resounds higher up in the mountain and comes down the slopes tumbling torrents of clay and pebbles— the cabin roof becomes the base of a cataract whose foam, when it touches ground, bounces back in dusty tears to the embers, where it evaporates with a sigh.

He turns the game as well as he can on its improvised skewer, set on the brick edges of the fireplace, spotted with muddy rain— the racket is terrifying; everything seems as if it's about to give way under the pressure of the storm—the cabin, the roof, the mountain itself, riddled like a machine-gunned body,

hunger ties your entrails in knots, blinds you, deafens you like this downpour, exterminating from under the heavens any flesh that still has the breath of life,

now it's the hail banging, it rings out like snipers training on the corrugated metal roof, ding, ding, ding, suddenly the air is freezing, the hailstones bounce up to a meter in the air, they accumulate in hollows and crevices, the spectacle is so powerful that for an instant he forgets his birds on the embers,

anything that had a breath of life in its nostrils is perishing, it's snowing shards of glass, splinters of ice—except except snow is soft and slow this hail is pure violence it leaps and scratches, a pack of mad dogs

thunder and lightning slash the darkened sky, the clouds hunch their shoulders,

he sits down under the porch on the stone of the threshold and eats as he watches the hailstones revert to rain beating down in the wind that has risen—the juice of the burning-hot fowl runs down his throat and onto his hands, he could cry from pleasure,

your father cooked skewered birds like this, on a wood fire, the products of his hunting, your mother, amused, watched the man take his place on that day,

amused with tenderness and respect,

dinnertime,

you can see your mother again modestly hiding her mouth with her hand to take out one of those tiny bones that always got stuck in the teeth,

the war has distanced all these moments, has pushed them back to the point of disappearing, how long ago was that, how long,

you're the age of one who is ageless,

grown white and coarse, you've waged war for three years, three years is nothing, 1,200 days maybe just as many corpses,

he chews on the last little bones while watching the rain, listens to the storm, to keep from thinking, again the thunder is tearing apart the mountain and the lightning is whistling like shells, he takes off his soldier's jacket, washes his mouth and hands under the downpour, the water drips onto his temples, forehead, chest, it's a kind of happiness that's a little frightened, a little careful—here you experience the childlike happiness of rain, the sky that opens up too much or not enough.

This solitude is so perfect, sitting on the ground, in the aromas of clay and the sounds of the water falling from the roof,

could you stay here, wait for the war to end, wait for peace, lost in the midst of the mountains, with no neighbors, no parents, no memories? Memory is a downpour to be driven away, inner hailstones,

he sits down crouched against the wall, like a soldier in a corner
of the barracks courtyard,
   the rain has stopped,
   the wine-colored sky is sinking into evening.

The donkey limped, then fell onto its side in the devastation, the debris of wood still smoking despite the rain, the oak leaves sticky with blood against the fainting woman—her dress torn by the lightning, her white skin blackened and reddened, her mouth gaping open. Then the donkey got up and fled, it ran down the slope like a drunken, panic-stricken man, swaying its neck, it staggers on the path, limps, brays, almost falls at each step setting off an avalanche of pebbles, it follows the same path it came on, its black coat stained with dark spots like a bull after it's been lanced, its head nearly touching the ground—it hurtles down the mountain, moved by fear and pain, it wants to run away, find the stable again, the refuge, hay, care; thirst swells its tongue, a vermilion blood oozes from its nostrils.

Its feet tremble with suffering, fear makes a tear stream from the edge of its blind eye, terror reinforces its single-mindedness: it runs toward the valley like a mad thing, almost collapsing at each step.

He took the gun apart to stave off boredom in the agony of the day. Played with the long spring, cleaned the barrel with the metal rod, oiled the moving parts—he can see almost nothing now, the moon hasn't risen, only Sirius is shining in the still-bare sky.

He'd like to have the luck to come across a hare,

tomorrow at dawn you'll go back to hunting,

wait all day for a furtive movement, avoiding thoughts, keeping your mind blank,

you have to contemplate the future, you can't stay here hiding in the house until the end of days or the end of the war,

you deserted, if they find you they'll hang you or slit your throat,

you've joined the camp of the conquered, the camp of never-ending flight,

he watches the constellations as they're printed on the tar of the sky, the air again smells of flowers, the rain is moving away— suddenly he hears snorting, trampling, heavy breathing, an animal is there; with a little luck a roe deer, a wild goat, a boar even, he seizes his rifle, stands up as quietly as possible, he's a tall shadow darker than night behind the little wall,

one eye the sheen of porcelain, a bluish moon,

the donkey is back,

the woman must not be far away, the woman or whoever stole her donkey,

he quietly loads the rifle and crouches behind the wall, invisible in the darkness, he hears nothing but the donkey stumbling about, breathing, moving, no human footsteps. His feet bare, hunched low, he walks around the cabin, slowly, listening to the night, he looks out over the shack, tames the shadows, nothing moves except the animal, he goes back down on the other side behind the animal, which takes a few steps back, frightened,

come here, idiot, what happened to you, you look like you've come back from the front,

its coat is burned in patches, it has cuts on its flanks, it's bristling with splinters, its tail is severed and bleeding, its ears are mangy and blackened, cut as if with a scissor, its hocks all chewed up, its tongue is hanging out, blood is dripping from its mouth,

and the dark is no doubt hiding other wounds. He fills the tin basin and brings it to the donkey, trying not to frighten it, then he moves away, the animal drinks noisily.

He didn't hear any bombing or shell-firing, nothing that could explain the animal's disastrous state—an explosion or a fire, its owner must be dead, a mine maybe, perhaps she set off a powerful mine and the donkey was behind her, but there are no mines in the mountain, what would be the point, no mines or tanks, no mortars, no cannons, no planes either during the storm,

aside from the storm itself, but you can't believe that, fire from the sky doesn't shoot down like that onto the earth,

lightning is a distant presence,

it only frightens animals and the simple-minded.

He goes over to stroke the prone donkey, the animal is breathing deeply, its eye open, its head on the ground, its nostrils and mouth are crusted with blood—a childlike sadness overcomes him, the donkey will die, and yet it kicks and tries to bite when it's touched, it's suffering, even lying down it's suffering,

you could kill it, you'd just need one bullet, barrel against skull, put an end to its sufferings, but you've put an end to too many sufferings,

eyes closed or wide open,

the donkey will stay in the night, in darkness and solitude.

XIV

Paul Heudeber always maintained that the form of *The Buchenwald Conjectures* (those free verses, those disjointed phrases, the very personal syntax) was due to the size of the strips of paper on which he noted them down—a form that Paul preserved when he transcribed them in 1945. He didn't want to *rewrite* the *Conjectures*, he wanted to keep what they bore witness to, that is, the concentration camp experience. "To pursue my mathematical explorations, all I needed was a piece of wooden pencil and a little hope. But the more I wrote," he said, "the more I noted down, the more this hope allowed me to advance in developments that gave me every time more strength to continue. I had become these scribbles—or rather, I was floating somewhere between these scribbles and my starving body. But all that was possible because I wasn't among the most pitiable in the camp. I was protected by my comrades, I was working inside, I was surviving more than others."

Paul almost never mentioned Buchenwald—he barely named the camp, he said "on the Ettersberg," the name of the famous hill north of Weimar where Goethe went for walks and where the concentration camp was erected in 1937. The camp was supposed to be called Ettersberg, but the toponym was associated too much with Goethe and Schiller—the camp of the beech tree forest, Buchenwald, is a strange kind of euphemism; Goethe must not have any blood on his hands. Or rather: Goethe must not be defiled, even with a dozen years' distance, by contact with the filth of that communist, homosexual pigsty. The memory of Goethe and Schiller was not tarnished, or almost not. Just a little.

For Paul, Buchenwald was "the camp," "the camp on the Ettersberg," emptied, in the few stories he could share with me, of the suffering, the hunger, the disease. Paul Heudeber was invited to all the commemorations; he was present at the ceremonies of the fiftieth anniversary of the liberation in 1995; he was invited to the inauguration of the Memorial built by the GDR in 1958; in April 1963, in Berlin, he attended the premiere of the film *Naked Among Wolves* adapted from the novel by Bruno Apitz, his communist party and camp comrade, a film that tells the story of the organization of the communist resistance inside Buchenwald through the fate of a Jewish child found in a suitcase whom the resistants manage to hide from the guards—three or four years later, one evening when *Naked Among Wolves* was on TV, when I was a teenager, maybe fifteen or sixteen years old, I asked my father what he thought of the film: he replied that the camp was like the film, and the film was like the camp; then he hesitated a moment, before shaking his head and bursting into laughter. Forget this film, he said. We were all much dirtier, Irina, you know, much uglier. We were violent, stinking things, we were tortured all day and all night, and it's impossible to show that in a film, a world become suffering.

Naked Among Wolves is an example of what could be called the aporia of communist resistance: should the child be saved, if this act places the entire resistance organization in danger? But what's the point of a resistance organization, if it can't save a child? Bruno Apitz saves the child in his novel, and the film does the same. The Camp (Buchenwald) had become a key moment in the symbolic construction of East Germany, the construction of the regime's antifascist display case; the moment when, in the most painful heart of Nazism, within the organization of communist resistance in Buchenwald—those who will become the spearheads of subsequent antifascism, the ideological force of the Democratic Republic of Germany—the country still to come was metaphorically born in a child, a child who must be protected, for he represents hope. The memory of Buchenwald was always at the heart of the GDR: among the communist comrades detained at the same time as Paul in Buchenwald were a number of senior members of the subsequent East German intellectual elite;

communist resistance in Buchenwald became one of its founding myths—after some hesitation, it's true, in Stalin's lifetime: Ernst Busse, one of the leaders of communist Resistance in Buchenwald, died in deportation, this time in a Stalinist camp. Paul's friend, Walter Bartel, also a communist, who would become a historian specializing in, among other things, Buchenwald, was an object of investigation by the Party and was for a long time kept away from power. Not Paul, as far as I know.

So Paul Heudeber can be found in history books in two different ways, as a communist concentration camp survivor summoned to high-level responsibilities in the GDR on one hand, and as a brilliant mathematician on the other—these two qualities tending, as must happen, with the years, to be erased in human memory to the point of near-disappearance: over thirty years after the end of East Germany, the characters (as personalities go) who inhabited it are nothing more than extras in a slightly kitsch film, usually a spy film. The many appearances of my father's name in the credits of the "Umschau" and then the "Aha" East German TV networks are forgotten—his role as revealer, so important for him, of science within everyone's reach, he who so often shouted "to do physics or biology you need laboratories, money, whereas to make breakthroughs in math you just need a library, intelligence, and rivalry." Math was portable; you could keep the question's phrasing more or less in your head. You could emigrate with your theorems, your hypotheses, your laboratory on your back, as Emmy did. You could easily and at very little expense cover the globe with a network (Paul said "a galaxy") of Institutes of Mathematics, which would draw its strength from the young people of decolonized countries that achieved freedom and joined antifascist forces. Paul had also been a pedagogue, an instructor, a great dreamer about the universality of knowledge. All his life, until the end of the GDR, Paul had tried to endow East Berlin with a major, centralized mathematics library—he pestered the authorities, fought like a lion, because he was fed up with being forced to run all over Berlin several times a day to find an article in a mathematics journal, half of whose issues were in one spot, the other half in another, etc.; at the time it would have made more sense to go to Warsaw to spend a week at the mathematics study center, Warsaw or Prague, instead of spending an hour on the streetcar to get a document that in the end couldn't be found: it would save time. Paul dreamed of an Institute of Mathematics, a real research center where all branches would be represented— algebra, algebraic geometry, topology, number theory, but also statistics, probability, calculus, algorithms ... Which he never managed to obtain.

I realize how hard it is for me to avoid panegyric when I write about my father, and how easy it is to plunge into a kind of ironic, annoyed criticism when I talk about my mother. Both my parents were such powerful models that I could do nothing but escape, flee, find in distance—the past, exotic languages, remote coun- tries—a place to exist. Despite all that, I never really left either the Schlossstrasse, or Maja, or Paul.

Maja always remains mysterious.

The last twenty years have passed quickly. The war is back. The epidemic preceded it. I celebrated my seventy-first birthday.

I view these last weeks completely enclosed in the memory of my parents, as if I were stuck in the twentieth century, unable to extricate myself from it.

I devoted my doctoral thesis to the algebra of Omar Khayyam, then my accreditation thesis to the question of irrational numbers in Nasir al-Din Tusi. I learned Arabic in Cairo. I took refuge in the heart of the Middle Ages the way you leave your native village to try your luck in a distant city. Cairo was at once the capital of archeology, of ancient knowledge, the city of the Fatimids and the Mamluks, and the Metropolis of Nasser and Sadat. Cairo smelled of the Nile, of decomposition, jasmine, sweat, and boiled beans. Paul was disappointed that I was devoting myself not to pure mathematics, but to its history; Paul was disappointed that I wasn't the first woman to finally win the Fields Medal; Paul didn't see how present he'd been in my career choices, even though it wasn't obvious. Despite my flight and my remoteness, the fruit hadn't fallen very far from the tree.

The first woman to receive the Fields Medal was in 2014, finally, twenty years after Paul's death, an Iranian, Maryam Mirzakhani, a descendant of Tusi and Khayyam: her work was a continuation of Paul's, the geometry of Riemann surfaces; I don't know if she was familiar with Paul's book (beyond the theorems and developments that are now part of shared mathematical heritage): I know only that, in an autobiographical text, Maryam Mirzakhani explains that when she was a child, she dreamed of being a writer. Maryam Mirzakhani died of breast cancer at the age of forty, just three years after receiving the award that the entire mathematical world dreams of—an immense sadness overcame me, at that moment, I'd have willingly given years of my life to prolong hers, though I knew almost nothing about her.

*

Maja visited me three times in Cairo (pyramids of Giza, Alexandria, Luxor, Aswan), Paul, never. Reading over our correspondence I came across this paragraph:

My dearest Irina, please excuse my lack of passion for obelisks, temples, sphinxes, rivers, feluccas, Gods, Goddesses, hieroglyphs, deserts, oases, and camels. I'll see you in Berlin instead, will you come back for New Year's?

I was extremely annoyed, of course, but I said nothing. I confided in my mother—I'm furious with Papa, I can still hear myself uttering that phrase, as we were going up the Nile under sail in the company of a group of tourists. We'd just passed the Nilometer; we could see, high up on the right bank, the walls of Old Cairo behind the dusty banyan trees, the unreasonable mango trees, the offended palm trees, and the English buildings on the Corniche that were reflecting the setting sun as it was sinking far away over there in melted brown-gold toward Mohandiseen, at that moment when all of Cairo seems to be holding its breath before uttering the call to prayer in unison, that sudden breeze swelling the sails of the feluccas and speeding their movements in the bluish darkness of the Nile. I'm furious with Papa, that was a little girl's phrase, on the deck of that Doric sailing bark being maneuvered by an elderly gentleman in a turban, whose dark olive face showed no emotion, none, neither pleasure nor displeasure, completely impassive, with the tiller under his right armpit. Opposite us, on the other side of the deck, was an Anglophone family, Canadians or Americans. Maja, as usual, was attracting all the light—tall, beautifully made, her curves, her air of elegance, the assurance of her low voice, always made her the center of attention: in this man's world of Cairo, and despite the austerity of her appearance, she won the hearts of everyone, from the ticket agent at the Ramses train station to the receptionist at the Hotel Osiris. I'm furious with Papa, he could have come with you, and Maja took my hand as if I were still a child, her child, You can't be mad at him, how could you think he'd leave Berlin, even if only for a few days? To be with you, the three of us, he might have gone to Warsaw,

Frankfurt even, but Cairo, that's not his world. He's working very hard just now, too. He misses you very much, he's hoping you'll come back to Germany for a little this winter, and the evening sun, the *shams el aseel* that Umm Kulthum sings of, redrew my mother's face, erasing her shadows, dazzling her with youth. She had just turned sixty.

Maja did not share my passion for classical mathematics in Arabic, but she had loved Egypt, especially the Valley of the Nile, that Upper Egypt of peasants on their narrow, fertile green strip so abruptly bounded by desert. Antiquity didn't interest her much; we had bicycled for kilometers around Kurna, on the left bank, opposite Luxor, in the midst of fields — Maja's passion was for the work of the architect Hassan Fathy, whose manifesto, *Architecture for the Poor*, had been published a few years earlier. We had visited the mosque in the New Gourna Village, along with a few homes; Maja was determined to make his work known in Germany, she kept wanting to involve the Ministry of Foreign Affairs and international cooperative agencies. For Maja, the work of Hassan Fathy represented the future; he used the oldest and simplest knowledge in matters of construction — the Nubian vault, roof terraces, brick — to return to an environment that was not only truly local and adapted to the needs of the inhabitants but above all inexpensive, easy to build with native materials, and, in this period of the late 1970s when no one was remotely interested in ecology or in sustainable development, Maja had the intuition, in this welcoming warmth of the upper Nile valley, that something unique was at issue here, an example for what was then called "the Third World."

In Germany, all anyone could talk about was the Red Army Faction, plane hijacking, suicides in prison, and I was quite happy not to have to discuss all these matters with my father Paul Heudeber: in Cairo they only talked about Peace, travel to Jerusalem, economic development, opening up; we could sense something in the air. Impossible to suspect, of course, that this something was doomed to finish in blood under the submachine gun volleys of the Muslim Brotherhood three years later. Anwar Sadat was assassinated on October 6, 1981, and in early 1982 I was back in Steglitz and the Schlossstrasse; rather quickly I joined the Technical University of Berlin, much later Humboldt University, and then, even later, the Institute that my father himself had led for years, through a kind of *a posteriori* endogamous nepotism that could just as easily be called *chance*. It is well-known that chance always leads us back to ourselves.

Omar Khayyam's algebra, that is, the *maqala, al-jabr wa al-muqâbala*, was a daily source of wonderment. The use of conic sections to solve cubic equations, or "the equivalence of a cube with squares, sides and numbers," as Khayyam writes, seemed to me to be worth all the suns of Cairo. My teachers patiently taught me the scientific terms and syntax; I learned a little Egyptian dialect, and remembering that today makes me want to jump onto an Egypt Air flight to Cairo — the "Paul Heudeber Days" unfortunately did not take place on an *'awwâm*, a riverboat moored to the banks of the Nile, but on the *Beethoven*, opposite Peacock Island, in Berlin: I think, however, that if Maja had insisted, Jürgen Thiele would have bent over backwards to transport everyone to Cairo, in a contemporary version of *Chitchat on the Nile*, the fluvial novel by Naguib Mahfouz.

XV

He'll try to sleep, on the stone bench, in the cabin, almost naked, wrapped in the cool of darkness, the sun will rise very soon, arms under his head he tries not to think, here in the land of childhood it's childhood that rules, childhood that decides,

you can see yourself again stretched out just the same, as a boy leaning against your father,

his black hair against your black hair,

on the stone bench in the shack,

the war was nothing but a distant, foreign monster then,

your father would take your hand and together you'd climb up to the cabin, everything was alive, cultivated, harvested, olives would be beaten down in December, when they were purplish-red in the tree, they'd fall onto a tarpaulin that then became a sack, the olives went to the press except the ones your mother plunged into a basin, and washed, and washed, before letting them rest in salt and bay leaves, you can still summon to your mouth the savory taste of the bay leaves, and the oily bitterness of the olive, the solar miracle of lemon—all those tastes announced Christmas, the end of autumn, all that hinted of winter, the cold, the snow that sometimes fell higher up in the mountain and that you'd go to see, you'd climb up to see the snow and even touch it, up there, and you'd come back down to the cabin, to the edge between worlds, between the world of hills, villages, and school, and that of the high places, stones, and wind: your father would snatch you away from the universe of discipline and boredom of school to carry you to the fierce magic of nature, snakes, and birds of prey,

you'd run toward your secret places, your hideouts, your treasures, you'd run toward the little grotto of the spring, you'd run toward the salamanders, the lizards, the shiny, bulbous beetles that you'd flush out from between the stones, toward childlike heroism faced with black garter snakes, spiders, scorpions,

nothing frightens the male child, terror is swallowed whole, it grows inside you, it's a seed of virility,

the father's love was measured by the fear endured,

by the pain endured,

you have to suffer to protect the things that belong to you, the huts, the fields, the wells, the mothers, the sisters,

God is a demanding father,

on the stone bench in the cabin.

He spares a thought for the donkey, outside, and for the woman, he searches his memory for her in a village street, on a square, they weren't enemies, then, just neighbors, and this nearness was mottled with jealousies, mistrust, scorn, before it was streaked with insults. They didn't dance at the same parties, didn't applaud the same speeches; the war sliced through shared life, the life of fathers, brothers loaded into trucks, buried in mass graves,

others by your hands,

others—and

and enemies of the Homeland were forced to pay up,

he turns over on the stone bench, he is cold,

that's how the inevitable explodes, not with a huge bang but in a bloodthirsty fissure, it becomes filled with blood till it overflows,

and all the faults and all the ditches fill with blood,

all the crevices, the lines and borders boil with blood they're torrents, rivers with forgotten floods that suddenly carry death along, the street that separated us from our neighbor is filled with death, the roads we took into town transport death, the squares, the parks in which we shouted for joy are decked with the colors of death,

you close your mind to memory the way you lower your eyelids,

the cabin closes in on you and protects the animal in its hole.

God I beg you,

she is so weak that she can't stand up, move even, she's trembling, her flesh is moving despite herself, she's agonizing in a dense, infinite suffering of the night sky—she's so sick, so thirsty that she drinks from the pebbles pressed against her face, so softly, and these traces of rain under her lips give rhythm to her moments of unconsciousness, her gaps in awareness, which link evening to night and night to day, the burning of dawn with the torture of awakening,

I can't breathe, I can feel the fire of dawn on my skin,

she imagines the donkey, stretched out also not far from there, the tree still burning in the morning, she doesn't have the strength to groan anymore, all this will soon be interrupted, will melt into deep blackness. She doesn't hear the rustling sounds of the mountain, she no longer smells the fire mingled with the scent of earth, she squeezes her fist in pain and at the injustice of it, she is afraid, she is an animal crushed with suffering on the wet ground, one last rhythm that holds back her soul, one beat, the regular beat of solitude, hope is nothing but a handful of seconds in the open hand of agony, when you count at daybreak the spots on the sun of death, when you reject that last face so you can kiss dawn's patch of cloth, spotted with stars and regrets,

she follows the thin line of comfort, the expanses of metallic water rippling with gentle waves,

my mother stroked me gently, when I was a child,

she'd like to slip away but her sticky body is spread out on the meager silt from the storm, the earth, slimy with fallen water, surprised by the darkness of venous blood: her body is holding her prisoner, she sinks into a moment without memory, she descends into a thicket of fog, with scarlet streaks of pain; God is there, somewhere; God is in the folds, the gatherings of matter, God is biding His time, God is an animal on the alert,

God is waiting for the angels of night to join the angels of day to pray.

XVI

The day before the opening of the conference, on Monday evening, before dinner at the White Owl inn on September 10, 2001, Jürgen Thiele, who was at the time, as I mentioned before, general secretary of our Berlin Institute, had confided his anxiety and sadness to me—his sadness, he said, that Paul was no longer with us, his anxiety at guessing that Maja didn't seem very happy with this seminar. He seemed to be regretting, while not daring to say so, that he'd given in to the futilifugal forces (research laboratories, partner universities, foundations, Maja) that had urged him to "transplant" our activities onto a boat in Wannsee. This support from the University of Potsdam is very good, but I'd feel better if we were on our own premises in Berlin—all this is a little strange. I remember trying to reassure him, Spree or Havel, it's six of one, half a dozen of the other, after all it's a math conference, that's what matters, whether it takes place on the Seine, the Rio de la Plata, or the Nile, even in front of Bernini's Fountain of the Four Rivers in Rome! The mention of Rome elicited a smile from Jürgen—he put a finger across his lips, as if to say, "Don't give your mother that idea," which made me laugh in turn.

In the rustling air of the Brandenburg border, on the last evening before the catastrophe, was there something that might have led us to imagine what was about to happen the next day? Linden Pawley was dining opposite my mother and seemed wholly charmed by Maja and her carmine lipstick. After we left the restaurant, I stayed for a while on the deck of the *Beethoven*, leaning against the rail facing the shadows of Peacock Island, alone with my sadness and my wool sweater. For some months, ever since I'd turned fifty, I'd been struggling with images of death. I imagined I was going to die soon. My father's so-sudden end haunted me.

My solitude, even though I had chosen it myself and accepted it, was an immense echo chamber for my sadness, where melancholy resounded, amplified until it became profound unhappiness.

The *Beethoven* was softly creaking in the night, I couldn't keep myself from thinking about the 1940s, Paul's arrest, his tortured body; the groans of the hawsers rubbing their strands against the metal of the mooring cleats were extremely sinister.

XVII

He observes the catastrophe, she might feel his eyes on her body, he remembers so well the violence he has inflicted that no surprise alters his face, no pity, no compassion; he sees the black, broken leg, he sees the wood buried in flesh, he sees the immense bruise on the ribcage, the torn shirt, the white skin striped with sorrow,
you should end it,
he has the rifle with him, what else is there to do, soothe, hasten, finish what is already underway, she wouldn't realize, she has fainted, he'd just have to bring the barrel close to her ear, an explosion much less obtrusive than the one that ripped open the tree behind them, the holm oak is nothing now but two black, jutting pieces of bark, two hooked fingers of a monster accusing the sky in an obscene V. He surmised the storm, he imagined the lightning, which explains the burns on the donkey's coat, the splinters, the wounds, the donkey had followed him as well as it could into the mountain, they climbed one behind the other into the bed of the torrent where the storm scattered its rivulets.
He thought he'd find a body already gnawed by vultures and birds of prey.
He doesn't know why he climbed up here, why he followed the donkey or why the donkey followed him—he bandaged the animal that morning as well as he could, gave it water to drink, the donkey kicked, brayed when the man tried to touch it,
brayed, kicked, bit,
it had regained its strength,
the old one-eyed donkey was limping, it was hobbling on three feet.
Maybe the donkey too was curious, maybe it wanted to know—

it had to climb up the mountain to understand, the way the man needed to hunt.

The rifle is on your shoulder, you just have to make one move to put an end to this story,

one more time,

he leans toward her, he'll leave this useless body to its death throes,

pull the trigger, pull, finish her off,

why shoot at what is already on the ground,

she is not prey,

he has given this coup de grâce to bodies still very much alive that didn't know they were dead, their eyes blindfolded, their bodies that fell heavy and dull into a ditch,

in the beginning of the war,

women, children, peasants, teachers, at daybreak they took on a sickly complexion when they were covered over with earth, the earth that shifted in his nightmares, undulated on the surface, as if peopled with monsters, with worms slithering through death and the frenzy of war.

He doesn't know the causes of his actions, he doesn't know why he does what he does, why he acts, to what purpose, by what means, what heavenly motivations or earthly machinations move his sullied hands, my God, can there still be in Thee a tiny particle of goodness that we haven't squandered—from the flask he cleans the woman's face, moistens her lips and face,

if you don't finish her off she'll take a long time to die, days maybe, until she dies of thirst,

he didn't kill her yesterday, he won't kill her today, neither her nor the donkey nudging its mistress with its muzzle.

Is the war over, is desertion dwindling to cowardice, he looks at the donkey, its torn ear, its white eye of veined marble, its neck blotched with burns, the sun is high up in the intense blue of spring, the air is budding with flowers and rustling with perfumes. A pale scent is rising from the ground.

Abruptly, he pulls out the wooden lance stuck in the woman's thigh, but the atrocious pain caused by this sets off no movement, no bleeding aside from a few dark drops on the muscle's pink flesh, against the gray of the bone deep in the wound. He unwinds the strip of cotton around the thigh, roughly, tries to close up the wound, knots the cloth.

He wonders if the donkey is strong enough to carry her.

He could make a stretcher with two branches, his jacket and pants as canvas, but he'd have to drag her to the cabin through the stones from the stream, impossible. There are no emergency services to wait for; in the mountain there's no network, no phone, no electricity, no railroad that can carry the dead body. He'll have to abandon her to the foxes and wild vultures.

He places his hand on the woman's neck to feel the blood beating in the carotid. War and torture have taught him all he knows about anatomy, all he knows about women. The skin is warm; he squeezes her throat a little between his fingers, the pulses are transmitted to his own blood, she is alive,

you alone know the fragile stubbornness of this life,

I feel a touch on my throat,

she imagines she's jumping up, she wakes to pain as to a blinding light,

a thick tar in my lungs keeps me from breathing, I'm thirsty, I have a sandy thirst in my mouth, a thirst of earth, of terror, she imagines she's moving, crawling, writhing in anguish like a snake,

she imagines she opens her eyes,

I glimpse the sparks of a fire lit by suffering, fleeting stars streak my cornea with crimson,

a burning nausea crushes me against the earth.

The donkey brays suddenly, it's a bassoon; she feels her body break into pieces of fire, into sparks of lava when she's lifted from the ground, she utters a barely audible groan, she utters a rumbling from her throat before fainting again and going back to dreams red as velvet curtains, tense with terror and memories.

Prof. Dr. Paul Heudeber
Elsa-Brändström-Str. 32
1100 Berlin Pankow

Maja Scharnhorst
Heussallee 33
5300 Bonn 1

Maja your absence is not just a lack — it's causing the most intimate
kind of tension, a void that deforms the world around it. Time,
taste, the curves of light, the trajectories of thought — everything
is transformed by your absence; sometimes I walk, overcome with
an aimless energy; often I stay expressionless, motionless, letting
night fall around me and leaving my work table (where I've done
nothing but look out the window) to go to bed, without a sound,
without saying a word. Every morning the daylight returns to remind me — to remind me of what? Then I walk, I leave Elsa-Brändström-Strasse as soon as I awaken, I wander around Pankow to
a lake, which I walk around, I walk to another lake, I tire myself
out, I walk until I'm faint with hunger, faint with thirst, faint with
exhaustion, but no, I walk as I let the daylight sink around me
when I sit down and every second of thought, every spark of my
senses is turned toward you, toward our memories: the low, red
sun of the winter sunset, my hands in yours, my arms around you,
our faces touching, then there's nothing but your breath that's
intoxicating Berlin, the gray of the sky is your breath, the vapor
on the water is your breath, your mouth the river, your hands a
burning-hot earthenware stove. You become the metallic odor of
coal, you become the basement, the stairs, the light at the top of the

stairs, you become the door, the table, the basket on the table, the telephone, the Bakelite of the telephone, the night falling around me, the darkening window, the hope of sleep.

I've been thinking a lot about Liège these days—why, I don't know. The room at the landlady's house on the cul-de-sac. The Outre-Meuse. The extraordinary welcome of the Communists of Liège for whom we were refugees who needed to be helped. You, shivering with cold in my arms and the damp sheets in the garret. The meat stews, the soups, the river. The strolls through the hills, our returns to the garret, the river. Studying, the river. I was finishing the articles on Hilbert and especially on Emmy. I missed Emmy. I felt as if I were summoning her by applying myself to her work. Making her appear like a goddess. The way the goddess spoke to Ramanujan. We didn't want to go back to Germany until the Nazis had disappeared. We didn't believe in the war. We thought Hitler would never dare. That France, Great Britain, the USSR would intervene before it was too late and destroy Hitler and his regime.

Maja, everything weighs on me, these days. Work. Solitude. Even math weighs on me. The students. We've opened a new area of research in statistics and computation, I know nothing about it and that irritates me. I've always hated calculations, and the people who do them even more.

Come on, join me. I know you'll tell me once more that you can't, that you have obligations, duties, that you're suspected of spying for the enemy, who knows what else.

But never mind. Since you are everywhere, I don't need you anymore, my love lives without its object. Even better: it has become its object, which is you, which is the world.

Paul

XVIII

Nasir al-Din Tusi, the great thirteenth-century Persian scholar, is not only a great philosopher, a brilliant mathematician, and a physicist equal to Galileo, but also a first-rate writer; we owe him a terrifying story about the destruction of Baghdad in 1258 by the Mongol armies of Genghis Khan's grandson, Hulagu Khan, under whom Tusi was a government minister. Tusi witnessed the destruction of Baghdad from the camp of the destroyers, the camp of those who piled up heads to make immense pyramids from them, who killed even the dogs, even the birds, it was necessary that nothing and no one survive; the perfect silence of victory had to reign over all.

Tusi had spent half his life in a fortress hidden in the folds of the Alborz range, in Kuhestan, a fortress named Alamut, which was the citadel of the Assassins, that "Ismaeli sect," as Orientalists called it. I remember the Nagel guide in Iran, published in 1967, said it took four to five days on horseback from the city of Ghazvin to climb up the valley of Shah Roud, the river of the King, and reach the castles of the Nizarite Shiites who were the masters of the region between the tenth and thirteenth centuries, until the arrival of those Mongols whose administration Tusi joined—it is probable that his reputation as a scholar had already reached Hulagu and his advisors: the head of the Mongol armies knew that in the citadel of the Old Man of the Mountain there was the greatest scholar of all time, the one who could decipher the movement of the stars in the heavens. Although no one really knew how or why, the scholar, the philosopher, the mathematician, the one who would become the best astronomer of his time, Nasir al-Din Tusi, joined the Mongol armies; Tusi accompanied the Mongols to the capital of the Abbasid caliphs, as far as Baghdad.

Baghdad of the House of Wisdom and the libraries, Baghdad of the *Thousand and One Nights*, Baghdad of thought, of poetry, of knowledge and poetry, Baghdad which had been the beacon of the world for five hundred years and was lost, destroyed by Hulagu's Mongols at the beginning of February 1258—how many died in the massacres that followed the fall, *all*, that is Nasir al-Din's reply, *all* died, the scholars and the illiterate, the wealthy, the poor, the powerful, the beggars, the women, the men, the slaves, and the Muslims: all were killed, their bodies piled up, they even killed, with arrows, the crows and carrion feeders that approached the corpses. Then Tusi went on his way, without shedding a tear, apparently, for the lives that had just been lost, nor for the science that was forever destroyed. As if he was certain it would be rebuilt. As if it was up to the scholars to rebuild. The great Saadi of Shiraz sings the threnody of Baghdad and the Caliph:

The sky itself weeps blood
On the kingdom of Mosta'sim
Last Commander of the Believers

I was thinking about the fall of Baghdad, on the afternoon and evening of September 11, 2001, opposite Peacock Island in Wannsee, in a kind of sad reverie, my head full of images of destruction in New York, unaware obviously that Baghdad would once again, a few years later, be destroyed. The *Beethoven* wasn't swaying any more than it had that morning during the conference's first session, solidly moored to the dock; the assembly room had slowly emptied, in a sort of decay, a withering away. At 6:30 p.m. we had decided to cancel what remained of the "Paul Heudeber Days." My mother was shocked, terrified by what she saw on TV; she was at a loss, she trailed after Linden Pawley in infernal, concentric circles; Pawley, whose daughter worked as an actuary in an office at the World Trade Center, was vainly trying to phone New York, to find out, to understand, to talk to his wife, to someone, to move forward his return plane ticket, and all these tasks came up against walls and, one after the other, turned out to be absolutely pointless: the American sky was completely closed to air traffic and all flights canceled. (Pawley ended up taking one of the first flights that went to the United States, just three days later, from Frankfurt, after spending, in vain, forty-eight hours at the airport hotel.)

The night kept falling.

The conference's afternoon session had been interrupted during the coffee break, after a doctoral student had presented his results relating to the calculation of the Haussdorff dimension for the Heudeber function and its consequences. We didn't know it then, but the discussions would never resume.

To escape the agitation, the objectless tension (we were thousands of kilometers away from the site of the catastrophe and yet we were acting as if the towers were there, next to us, as if we too were crushed under the rubble of shock), I went up to the deck—it was a beautiful late summer afternoon; the Havel was smooth and opaque, veering between watery green and glints of silver. It had rained all day, and now the sun was appearing.

I thought about our cruise of the day before; the world had changed, lives had been lost, as they are every day, but above all a part of our faith had collapsed with the towers—our faith in a kind of peace, of reparation, was crumbling away; already during the previous decade the wars in Yugoslavia had tinged with red the joy of the fall of the Wall; Europe had averted its eyes, people thought the Balkans were violent lands full of savages. Would Paul have shouted that only communism and fraternity could save mankind from its own fury, I have no idea.

I was leaning on the rail on the lake side.

The water had a smell, a plantlike smell.

Maybe Paul and Tusi were right, it was better to take refuge in the worlds of stars and mathematics—stars, love, bodies, rings, ideals, that whole hodgepodge of things so profoundly human that it cannot collapse, for it remains in us, in the imaginal world.

Suddenly, Jürgen Thiele was standing next to me. He too looked dejected, a little exhausted; it was 7:30 p.m. and the "Paul Heudeber Days" had collapsed with the towers. To console him, I had told him we'd organize another homage, in Mitte, this time, at the Institute we should never have left. I think I remember he gave a slightly forced smile. He looked at the landscape around us, his tall body sort of unfolded; he observed what could be seen of the forest and then, on the other side, the white castle with the two towers on Peacock Island. He asked me if I knew why Maja had wanted our meetings to take place on a boat. I replied that I didn't know.

"Maja and Paul lived on a canalboat in 1940–1941 in Liège, on the Meuse. They were hidden by a communist bargeman and his wife," Thiele said.

Paul had been arrested in Belgium a first time in 1940, interned by the French at the Gurs camp, near the Pyrénées, a camp he escaped from to go back to Liège, Maja, and living underground. He was arrested a year later by the Gestapo, imprisoned, tortured, and deported to Buchenwald at the end of 1941.

Jürgen Thiele nodded. Yes, that's it. And in Liège, they had lived first in a garret on a cul-de-sac in a neighborhood called "Outremeuse," then on a canalboat a few hundred meters from there on the Meuse.

"They were happy on that canalboat," he added.

I imagine that's the case for all children of celebrities and even for all children in general: people are always giving you information about your parents. Especially if you're a woman, it seems. Your father this, your father that. To the point that you doubt what he himself may have written, what he himself may have said; you are dispossessed of their reality.

Jürgen Thiele had thrown that phrase into the river the way you get rid of something cumbersome. Happiness. He left almost immediately, embarrassed, not looking me in the eyes. I pictured Paul and Maja standing just where I was, holding each other, looking at a different river.

I stayed another good hour on deck, trying not to think about New York, to rid myself of the sense of horror unleashed by the repeated images of the attacks, those clouds of dust invading the streets and pursuing the crowds of people to swallow them up, those shapeless monsters of thick, deadly spirals—among the most upsetting images were those of children in Palestine rejoicing at the catastrophe: even though that in itself was, unfortunately, not surprising, it added to the painful, melancholic sadness of the moment.

I'd have gladly locked myself up in my cabin, not to reemerge for two or three days; I even envisioned taking the first suburban train that went by, while I lost all interest in everything—my mother, Jürgen Thiele, the Institute, Kant, Pawley, everybody.

XIX

The woman is stretched out on the whitewashed stone bench in the cabin, in the primitive darkness of the cabin: he wipes a sponge—green soap, old-fashioned scents, of mustiness and child-hood—over her body to remove the dried blood, examine the darkening bruises. He didn't undress her completely; he took off what remained of her skirt and blouse, her skin is white, spotted with dark freckles, in places, on her shoulder, at the curve of her hips; he has shifted her to her side; he checks her breathing with his hand on her ribs, the ribs where the largest contusion is, black and burning hot,

you can't kill her now, you can't get rid of her now,
it took most of the day to get her down here,
it's almost night,
if she makes it through the night she'll live,
you know these things, torture taught you,
it will be a night of war without warmth or clarity, a night with-out any help, you'd like to be able to call someone, a doctor, an am-bulance, a nurse, but here everything's silent, in the mountain, the telephones, the signals, the signs, despite the seeming proximity of lights on the shore—you could disappear, take the path to the north with the donkey, leave the woman here in the cabin, in the sky only the Dog Star is managing to pierce through the clouds,

he can hear the rumbling of distant planes—the bombs smash the buildings into a dust of concrete and powerlessness, in which gray men and women wandered, their bleeding children in their arms, helmeted emergency workers in the endless screams of vic-tims and undulating sirens, in the unintelligible mass of pain, the steel rebars suddenly twisted into the void, fixed, rusty lances—terror was a gray fog of dust, terror spread in clouds, in cement over the living. Corpses decorated the rubble with colors, the blue of work overalls, the threads of red scarves, crushed with the bodies that wore them, the only brightness in the colorlessness of destruction—he remembers the foreign planes smashing the defenseless cities, he remembers the joy these deaths and collapses brought him,

you loved seeing the camp of chaos tremble, you loved hearing the enemy suffer,

from the threshold he looks at the lights on the coast, the night is climbing up to him—the purplish fringes of the sea are dying in the silence of distance,

you are hungry,

you are always hungry,

nothing can satisfy you anymore, not oranges, not almonds cracked on the threshold with a stone, not the little fowl, you rediscover hunger the way you rediscover fear, it is life returning and with it despondency, my God, make nature bigger, my God, give us immensity, the languid safety of immensity,

stars for nights of war.

He explores the woman's bags in search of food. The clothes smell of soap and bay leaves. The clothes are soft. The shirts tell of a different life, different from the one lying there on the stone bench in his cabin. Skirts. Wool underwear for the mountain cold. Photographs, papers, a book. A hairbrush, he pictures her untangling the brown locks now missing; a cardboard file folder, with needles and thread; some aspirin, a few charms, a little dark wood octagonal box lined with red felt containing a few pieces of jewelry, possibly gold; something he takes for a very fine, very sharp dagger, with no hilt, he doesn't know its purpose—he finds a cotton bag holding some bread, another one full of little cheeses, round as balls and covered in dried herbs—he bites into one of the balls of cheese, it's the salt that surprises him first, salt, thyme and the taste of goat, of slightly burned milk. He tears the bread with his teeth, crushes a ball of cheese inside it and goes outside to eat on the porch. The night is getting even darker; lighting the outside hearth now would betray his presence for a radius of many kilometers. No moonlight outlines the branches of trees, the walls; the donkey is invisible, it can be heard grazing on leaves, snorting, stamping its feet, drinking. The cheese, the bread, and then some water appease his hunger. He takes the rifle, puts it on his thighs—he's sitting cross-legged, his back against the stones of the cabin; the odor of cold ashes from the little porch fireplace soothes him. He thinks of his father, all of a sudden. The odor of the father's ashes, the odor of the father's wood, his odor of fuel oil, too, of coal and garlic. His mother, in his memory, smelled of soap like the woman's things, or flowers,

in your memory your mother smells of summer,

flowers, fruit, pastry, jam,

the war falls away from him like a leper's skin, he loses it, he'd like to tear the war out of himself like a dead scab—the rifle is still on his knees, though, the memories inside him, the woman's body lying on the stone bench is a response of the bodies he dishonored to death, one motionless figure for hundreds of dead. He plays with the cartridges like a child—the brass cartridge case, the little steel cone at its tip, pointed, perfect, he takes them out of the magazine, puts them back in,

the evenings are long and dark,

he's so unfamiliar with reading,

there is an old farmer's almanac in a corner, or a soft, dog-eared book, but the darkness is almost complete. No lamp, no candle. He goes back in. The night is rustling. It fills the hut. He sits down next to the stretched-out woman,

she is breathing deeply,

she is sleeping,

you placed a bag under her head like a pillow,

you can guess at her presence, asleep, her womanly curves and flesh,

you can hear her breath rising into the abolished space,

it's a breath of nothing,

the air rises, descends, it flows from the invisible and haunts you,

you hear nothing but her,
the animal in her, the beast in her, the living being in her,
the circular sound of life.
This subtle rustling breathes in shadow, thyme, ashes, and spits out the deep and bitter wilderness,
he hesitates to touch her,
what is this stretched-out woman awakening? What is this weakness of a woman lying on her back in the dark provoking, while he is motionless, his back straight, sitting on the same stone bench, the woman is breathing and shivering,
he can no longer see anything,
all overcome by blinded breath,
Dear God, give her assistance, guardian angels, return for us, most holy Mother of God, save us, save us, and he repeats the words without a sound emerging from his mouth, like a child, in fear, he was praying, he was praying in fear, he gets up, walks over to the woman, sits down so close to her, so close, that he feels the woman's warmth against his thigh, he puts his hand on her forehead, the sweat is warm, he wipes off the sweat with his hand, then wipes his hand on his jacket, he picks up the sponge that's gone green from rot, it stinks too much, he throws it into a corner, takes a shred of the woman's clothing: he strokes her forehead with the cloth, he knows he's caressing, her cheek, her neck, he gently moves the cloth over her skin. She is breathing slowly, he passes his hand through her short hair, so short, gently stroking her head, how long,
Dear God may Your holy angels come and keep us in peace,
he strokes the woman's thick skull, her neck, his hard hands grow warm from the gentleness, he gets up again, goes to the hearth, feeling his way along, he gathers some dried grass, some tobacco leaves, some twigs, and lights them, the yellow light rises up to the woman's face, to her body, her short hair, her arms under her head, shadows fill the cabin. He sits down, traces the light on the woman's face with his finger—shades her according to the movement of the flames, strokes her according to the movement

of the flames. There are freckles around her nose, thick lips over which he passes his thumb, her ears are narrow, he strokes her shoulder, the light wavers, projects shadows onto her still-covered chest,

she is warm and he warms himself from this heat.

[Handwritten note added in pencil: *from the Gurs camp*]

Maja Maja summer is almost here—in it I can see the sea, the fire that rises from it, which is like a blue spark in your eyes that catches, illuminates a face and it's you who appear, in the middle of misery, in the middle of all these stunned destinies, blown together by the war, Germans, Austrians, Spaniards, Republicans, Jews, Communists, Anarchists, miserable beings, and we all await victory and liberation—if they don't come, we'll run away ... We are not mistreated, here, the French are frightened and disorganized but not mean, they do what they can, we are fed, we are watched without really being guarded—every day a family carries away a Spaniard despite the wire fence, an abduction, right in front of the eyes of the French (if not from under their noses). Most of them are people from around here ... Here they call us "the Belgians," which gives me a good laugh, we're all German: some from Aachen, some from Cologne, some from the south ... Seized in Anvers, in Brussels, in Charleroi, then gathered together in Orléans with other Germans in France, "members of the enemy nation," thank you Monsieur Daladier, then transferred here, long hours of blind travel, most are comrades or sympathizers: you can recognize the Nazis (there are some) by their arrogance and their doglike faces ready to bite, they are at once cowardly and confident, they hide because there are some fine incidents, you find one from time to time with his face bloody, his nose broken, poor guy, he ill-advisedly fell against the wall of a shed, and right afterwards you see a Spaniard walking off whistling, hands in his pockets. The French are nobody's fool, they know very well that most of the prisoners are not their enemies but the Nazis' enemies.

There's only one thing I'm looking forward to: finding you again, my love. I pass the time as I can, I try to think about series of prime numbers, I think I can demonstrate by analysis an intuition that Euler had, about the relationship between the series of fractions of prime numbers and the harmonic series (forgive me, I'll explain, the harmonic series is the sum of the fractions of natural whole numbers, $1 + \frac{1}{2} + \frac{1}{3} + \frac{1}{4}$, etc. We know that both diverge and that—at least this is Euler's intuition—the first is like the logarithm of the second. Demonstrating this by analysis is arduous, to put it mildly). Emmy had encouraged me on this path. I can feel the thing within reach, and it's sweet to plunge into the world of numbers when, all around me, there is nothing but prison and a kind of long pain of absence. The fact that I do math fascinates my internment comrades (we're not detainees here, we're *interned*: a nuance that my level of French doesn't allow me truly to grasp). To pass the time, I fire off simple problems like a math professor—the eighty barracks comrades (Spaniards, Germans, Jews from all over Europe) amuse themselves trying to solve them. Here we keep paper (scarce) for letters: math is on the walls, with pieces of rock or coal! The story of Socrates showing a slave how to double the area of a square by starting with the diagonal of the original square was a big success. I imagine they'll wonder, when they dismantle this camp, why the boards are blackened with $y2 = 2 \times 2$, triangles, and hypotenuses!

The Spaniards are arriving from the war, they're seemingly stunned, dazed, some want to sign up in the French Foreign Legion to fight against the Nazis, convinced that the war in Spain will resume. In a few weeks, between those who are secretly going back to their countries, those who find work in nearby farms, those who sign up and those whom France is drafting by force as road menders or sappers, soon no one will be left. The French are funny: so convinced of their superiority, they're giving us classes on *the language of Molière*, personally I'd rather it be the language of Poincaré or Galois. There's also a post office in the camp and the food isn't as bad as you might think. There are rumors here that they'll soon start arresting German women and not just men, so be careful ...

I hope this letter reaches you—I'm placing all my hope in this envelope, which was offered to me willingly by a Spaniard in exchange for math lessons. If they only knew how bad I am at geometry! How far away Göttingen is ...

Maja my love we will win, we have the strength of the circle, the strength of the right triangle without which there is no circle, solid as two rings one inside the other, the invariance of the realm of passion ... I'd like to tell you so many things that I'm staying half mute. I'm sending this letter to Max's eatery, so your address won't show on it. I'm launching this letter northwards. I'll slip into it like a genie into the lamp. If you whisper these words tenderly, then rub the paper very gently against your chest, I will appear.

P.H.

XX

This letter of Paul's from the Gurs camp is one of my favorites among Paul and Maja's correspondence—the energy of Paul's youth, his passion, his pleasure in teaching the rudiments of math, his unfailing optimism, all this contrasts so strongly with Buchenwald, with the traces we have of Buchenwald in *The Ettersberg Conjectures*, one almost has the impression it's a different man, before the torture, before the despair.

The long sadness into which Paul plunged in the late 1960s very certainly kept him from finding the energy to move to the west, waiting always, always, in calm and melancholy, for the amelioration of the conditions of life, for the arrival of socialism, for happiness and Maja: shut away, Paul devoted himself to studying his "utopian spaces," which have since been called Heudeber surfaces—until he left his isolation ten years later, without having published anything important (these marginal works, a sort of mathematical aporia, verging on topology and algebraic geometry, would be of interest only, much later and partially, to the relatively recent discipline called "spectral geometry"). All my student years, especially my Egyptian years, Paul spent as a recluse in his apartment in Pankow; he had almost no more teaching duties. He saw Maja very little—once or twice a year, they would get together somewhere, in Prague, Paris, or Vienna. They were well over fifty. If they went on loving each other, or rather if they went on saying they loved each other, it was in absence. Maja was, with the SPD, at the height of her political career in the 1970s—deputy, vice minister, pioneer in the struggle for women's rights. There are very few letters from my mother, in the boxes that contain Paul's correspondence. Very few, and none from that era, aside from a lovely painted cardboard bookmark, with a pretty red silk ribbon,

a bookmark completely covered in Maja's writing, dated in pencil
Mallorca 1978 (maybe given as a gift for Paul's sixtieth birthday):

> Paul Paul Paul
> This object that you
> Will place in your books
> In your formulas
> And your mysteries
> You know I understand you
> Each in our own world:
> You transform it
> I transform it
> We each dream
> Identical dreams
> Each on our own
> Side of the world
> Like two
> Sleepers each
> Prisoner of
> Their closed eyelids
> *Puerto de Soller*
> *1978*

Were they together, in Mallorca, or were they each on their own
side of the world—who knows. Which world was Paul transform-
ing, we don't know that either.

"A life advances toward its end to gleam finally with the meaning it bears within it; until the very last word, the story winds toward a conclusion that illuminates it. The beautiful existence of Paul Heudeber perfectly illustrates this kind of story for me."

The person who had uttered these words was at the end of the table in the dining room of the *Beethoven*, sitting on one of the black folding chairs that the onboard staff had just added. I didn't know him; he had worked, apparently, for the Max Planck Institute of Mathematics in Bonn; he had brown hair gone gray, and he might have been the age of Paul or Maja; I just knew that he had a foreign accent and was a specialist in analysis, or more precisely in fractal objects, for he had told us, at lunch, about his work on the Heudeber dimension as criterion of fractality. Despite his pomposity, his remark proved (or implied) that he had been intimately familiar with Paul's life, which had been at the center of our conversation for a good hour already. This specialist in fractals whose foreign name eluded me at the time continued his tirade on Heudeber's "beautiful existence," which had the gift of getting on my nerves. Paul Heudeber was my father; hearing the fractal specialist hold forth on the so-called beauty of his life exasperated me. The fractal specialist had an entirely unpleasant mustache that he twirled as he spoke, as he had done during his improvised statement at lunch, which, added to his accent, at times made his statements unintelligible. There were about fifteen of us at table, all "members," in some way, of the "Scientific Community"; Maja was nodding as she listened to the specialist but I thought I could guess, from the movement of her fingers, from the way she had of playing with her ring, that she was just as irritated as I was, and I had the intuition that her irritation stemmed from precisely those words, *a conclusion that illuminates it*—the tragic end of the life of Paul Heudeber my father was shadowy, obscure, and could in no way constitute an illuminating conclusion, but the specialist continued to hold forth. I remember that Maja was knitting her brows with an expression—I couldn't tell if it betrayed an immense anger or the most profound incomprehension. I had to interrupt the specialist before this painful evening (already tragic, exhausting with anguish, for Linden Pawley, who had been walking in circles on the boat ever since early afternoon and would withdraw to his cabin only to reemerge five minutes later asking if there was any news) became truly unbearable.

What news could there be? The TV set up in the *Beethoven* kept showing the same images in a loop, a plane crashing in a cloud of fire, bodies falling from the windows, towers collapsing, crowds running to escape the impenetrable clouds of dust as if emerging from the gates of hell. Analysts and experts of all sorts succeeded each other onscreen, where everyone awaited the reaction of George Bush, who had been moved to a safe location in a place kept secret somewhere between Florida and the White House, where he might reappear to give a speech. The conversation passed without transition from Paul Heudeber and math to the attacks, New York, Islamism, and I felt targeted, almost embarrassed, whenever Afghanistan, Iran, or terrorism was brought up again. I remember a remark of one of the guests, who referred to the Middle East in these terms: "Those countries whose extreme violence has just changed the face of the earth, as if the free world were suddenly submerged by a wave of fire," himself from Yugoslavia, a Serb from Croatia or a Croat from Bosnia, I forget which: a few years earlier, all the violence in the world was unleashed in those lands, so close to here, and everyone seemed to have forgotten that, but not him; he knew it was *the Turks*, I remember clearly he used this word, the *Turks*, who were responsible for the collapse not just of the Towers, but of the world in general. *The Turks* (the coorganizer, Alma Sejdić, had immediately repeated the word) have nothing to do with anything over there of course, it's distressing, the Yugoslav suddenly looked annoyed, he tried to nuance his statement, but only managed to make it more confused. Maja was observing all these men with a dismayed look, there were only three of us women—Alma Sejdić, the doctoral student who had helped Jürgen Thiele organize the conference, my mother, and me—around this improvised table where everyone tried pointlessly to speak louder than their neighbor. I wanted to send all these fine folks off to bed, the way you do in summer camp. The graduate student (I remember her very dark hair and black eyes) seemed frightened by what she was hearing. She kept glancing around with fearful eyes—she had helped Jürgen set up this large table around which everyone had gathered, or rather all those who hadn't left, some to Munich, some to Berlin, some to Göttingen. It was almost seven in the evening. "The beautiful existence of Paul Heudeber perfectly illustrates this kind of story for me" had started speaking again, but I wasn't listening to him. Several subgroups had formed; at one end of the table, around the "beautiful existence" and his mustache, a few young or relatively young people; Jürgen Thiele was fiddling with his pen; he looked profoundly bored. In the middle, my mother, with Robert Kant on her right; opposite her, the Yugoslav and me; at the other end, a group of scholars of all ages, including a few colleagues from Berlin and two Frenchmen, who looked like self-confident Bourbakists (André Weil, one of the founders of the Bourbaki group, with whom Paul had corresponded for a long time, until the 1980s; Weil had spent some time in Göttingen with Emmy when Paul was a teenager) with some glasses of beer that the waiters and waitresses on board the *Beethoven* had kindly brought. The television was a little further away toward the boat's bow, where we had spoken earlier; Linden Pawley was circling around in front of the set, battling with the immense anxiety of imagining, somewhere in the middle of these images of war, the body of his daughter. No one dared approach him, except Maja, who got up from time to time to take him by the arm with infinite tenderness and gentleness, she'd rest her head against his, hold him close and continue talking with him in a low voice for a few minutes, looking at the TV with him, and then would come back and sit down with us, tears in her eyes. At around eight o'clock Pawley left for the Tegel airport; he was determined to get close to Frankfurt, from which most intercontinental flights left. He waved goodbye to us from a distance, from the car that was waiting for him on the quay; they'd gone to get his suitcase—when she returned, Maja had traces of tears on her cheeks, she made a sign to me with her hand: I realized I was her daughter, but that unlike Linden Pawley's, I was on board the *Beethoven*, and this little gesture, which might mean something like "don't move, fortunately you're here and not there" which she made before shutting herself away in her cabin for the rest of the evening was a way of thanking fate: signs of affection from my mother to me were so rare that it was my turn to have moist eyes and to immediately go up to the deck to take the air.

The sun hadn't set yet, it was coming close to the trees (willows, beeches, poplars) on the banks of the Havel. All at once it was lovely outside; a light breeze seemed to be carrying the sun's rays to me; Berlin was suddenly bathed in a great, warm, humid calm. I imagined the drinkers continuing to drink, the dancers to dance; I wondered if everyone already knew what had happened in New York. I thought about my father, about this strange, failed, floating homage. The prow of the *Beethoven* was pointing south, toward Gliniecke. I wanted to get off the boat, to untie its huge hawsers, push the bow with my foot and watch it float away toward Potsdam, then toward Brandeburg, join the Elbe and disappear into the sea, like Paul himself, like a funeral bark loaded with mementos, let it take them away—Jürgen Thiele, Robert Kant, all the math wizards, the physicists, the logicians, my mother—and I'd have gone back to Steglitz and eaten a grilled sausage when I got out of the train and I'd have slept like a baby to awaken twenty years later.

XXI

He gets up as soon as the first glimmers let him tell white from black. The dawn is quivering, pale, glazed with unknown stars and planets. He had dozed, one hand on the woman—first on the nape of her neck, then on her shoulder. He goes out to gather some fruit to squeeze. Some oranges. He senses she's going to wake up. The wound on her thigh isn't suppurating. The wound has no red around it, it's not inflamed, in a few days she might even be able to sit up on the donkey. If she doesn't die. If the donkey doesn't die. Sometimes, he remembers, you die later on if you've gotten too many wounds—at night, often. They used to take out from the cells the littered bodies of those who had died in the night.

He shivers. Stretches. He fills a bowl and drinks the sweet mountain water. The donkey is lying between the low wall and the tree, as if hiding from predators.

He sits down on the porch and enjoys the rustling silence that serves as a prelude to the birdsong.

He's going to have to leave. He'll make sure the woman will live, that she'll get better, and he'll leave, continue his way northwards, alone. The cabin is only a stopping place, like a farewell to childhood. A farewell to memories that climb onto him like insects at night. Scents, sounds. Images. He has to throw everything behind him, recollections make no sound when they fall. The more remote the war becomes, the more he wonders why he's fleeing it.

You've wrapped yourself without thinking in the shroud of peace,

your youth frightens you, it's no longer a force,

every day that distances you from violence makes you more fragile,

strips you bare,

your life begins in war but doesn't end there.

He goes back into the cabin with the first red gleams of dawn, the room smells of ashes and the breath of the woman. He walks over to her, strokes her forehead with the cloth, she's breathing more deeply, with more strength, he strokes her short hair, the light through the door illumines her face, he strokes her back,

she feels the hand on her back, what the hand transmits through her suffering, her throat is nothing but a stone on fire, her body is lava of pain without flames,

I'm lying on my stomach, I'm thirsty, I'm in pain, I'm thirsty,

she moves an arm,

she moves an arm,

she moves,

opens her eyes halfway—he stops stroking her with the cloth, I'm back in the cabin,

she tries to move, to sit up, nothing seems to have any effect on her numb body—each tremble of her muscle sets off a wave of pain, she can't help but groan,

I can hear myself,

these sounds emerging from herself bring her back to the world, suddenly she's silent, opens her eyes wide, she is in the light seeping through the door, the extremely golden oblique light, she closes her fingers over her own hand, she squeezes her fist and loosens it, iron pain is throbbing at her temples, she is nothing but thirst, burning heat, pain,

I'd like to get up, sit up, I'm suffocating,

she's an animal trying to escape drowning, she moves, shakes herself, he tries to calm her, her eyes are open, he helps her with infinite precaution to turn over, she rests on her side with her head on a bag,

the yard beyond the door is overflowing with bright sun, it's morning, the man is next to her, the dazzling brightness keeps her from seeing his monstrous face, he brought her back to rape her,

he wants to make me his slave, he's a ghoul in his cave, he's a hyena that hypnotizes you so he can eat you, the pain is too great, she closes her eyes for an instant, a minute, an hour, a day.

With the knife he cuts in half some oranges that he squeezes with his hand, he fills the tin pot, eats the pulp, the pith, then washes his face and splashes himself with freezing water—bare-chested, he dries out in the sun; he gave some water to the lame donkey, the donkey with the burned coat, the animal goes from tree to tree, from bush to bush, and eats whatever's within reach, young shoots, tussocks upraised by spring, purple harebells, ivy-leaved toadflax on the stones, the yellow inflorescence of the Lydia broom on the edge of the slope, its gray neck stretches up to the lowest branches or else rakes the ground to appease its hunger, it too is suffering, it walks alternately on four or three hooves, one foot in the air the way a deformed child might play a sinister hopscotch. The sun is halfway up,

you have the woman in your head,

you must leave,

but leaving and abandoning her even with a pot of orange juice is killing her, you should have killed her twice already, fate is show-ing you the error of your ways,

or not, fate is whispering to you that one must persevere,

save what you've saved and save yourself,

so powerful is the strength of this morning, this Lord you can-not look in the face.

XXII

Alma Sejdić (small, long brown hair, beautiful face, a little over thirty) was continuing her speech when I went back down into the cabin of the *Beethoven* on the evening of September 11, 2001; she was lecturing the old ex-Yugoslav logician on his racism and also expressing her own fears faced with Islamist terrorism from Afghanistan, Pakistan, or organizations like Al Qaeda.

The cabin of the *Beethoven* was as resonant as a bell, it seemed empty—all the chairs (aside from ours) and tables had been folded away; only the bar remained, motionless and distant, in one corner; suddenly you could see the parquet floor perfectly, as in a ballroom—the soft light of the setting sun, after it had rained for most of the day, sent deceptive rays through the portholes on the Peacock Island side, an orangey softness, amplified by the water of the Wannsee.

Alma Sejdić had a beautiful voice, a somewhat round face that made her look a little like a child, but a wounded child—I was daydreaming as I pretended to listen to Alma Sejdić explain how Muslim countries were the first to suffer from terrorism and Islamist fighters; I was thinking of Khayyam and Tusi, the bay windows of the *Beethoven* swelled with light like sails. All of a sudden I felt completely exhausted. The old man of "the beautiful existence of Paul Heudeber" was whispering something in his neighbor's ear; he seemed to be boiling, agitated, as if he was the keeper of a truth that must be expressed, must surge up like a fractal explosion to illuminate us. Jürgen Thiele opened his eyes wide as he listened; opposite me, the Bourbakists were chattering, talking about a tourist plane attack on the Eiffel Tower that had been foiled, but we couldn't find out if that was true or a simple rumor. The ex-Yugoslav logician was turning pale with rage to see himself prey to the indirect remonstrances of Alma Sejdić—he was a few years older than her, we were all wondering if they were compatriots, who knows, or rather ex-compatriots from clashing camps.

"The beautiful existence of Paul Heudeber" took advantage of a moment when the wave of conversations was ebbing: the Yugoslav had fallen silent with the crossed arms and furious look of those who will always be right, whatever the argument, whatever anyone says to them. The fractal specialist could now take the floor again, with that aged voice in which, it seemed to us, a southern European accent was circling—I would like to return to Paul Heudeber, he said, snapping to attention, to Paul Heudeber and the war, I knew Paul Heudeber in the camp. I have been, from afar, a friend of Paul Heudeber's since the 1940s. And I can certify that he was an exceptional being whose demise, as I was saying before, illuminates his entire existence, retrospectively. He had said "demise" solemnly, supporting his statement with a gesture of his hand waving in front of him, straight up and down, as if miming the blow of an ax. His mouth was a little twisted—it was this, more than the accent, which in the end was not easily definable, which made his words sound slightly inarticulate. His upper lip was covered by a thick white mustache, and the right part of his face, if you looked at him for long enough, remained completely motionless while the other side became distorted as the muscles moved, giving his expression something strange, bizarre, wild. The man might in fact be the age that Paul would have been, a little over eighty; I met Jürgen Thiele's eyes with an inquisitive look, he replied with a rather comic expression, one that, in a TV series, would have signified "no solution is rejected at this stage of the investigation." I gave a similar look to the coorganizer, who closed her eyes in a sign of agreement, but I couldn't really tell what exactly she was agreeing with. The elderly man didn't seem to see or understand the terrifying aspect of the destruction we'd been witnessing on the television since the early afternoon; he kept repeating the importance of Paul Heudeber's life and the conclusion that illuminated it, but one sensed he wished above all to talk about himself, that he'd come here so others would listen to him, and that he had no intention of going home until he'd been heard.

The participants, however, were leaving the *Beethoven* one after the other; they'd discreetly say their goodbyes, mostly just to Jürgen Thiele, and would climb up to the surface via the boat's main staircase.

The specialist in fractal geometric objects was talking about trees, the shapes of leaves, the geometry of nature, in an immense digression that stemmed from his friendship with Paul Heudeber but seemed to have trouble returning to it; for now he was mentioning certain works by Benoît Mandelbrot and the description of fractal geometric objects that had revolutionized his life as a geometrician. For him mathematics was a sense, like sight or hearing, and therefore a way to perceive nature.

One could feel a certain boredom creeping in among those present; the Bourbakists were looking at one another as if they wanted to leave, but didn't dare, the French are polite. Alma Sejdić was raising her eyes to the heavens. Paul had never talked to me about mathematics as a sense, but he could have. The old geometry specialist returned to Paul Heudeber in an unexpected way: Without him, I never would have come into contact with mathematics, he added. It was Paul who started this sense in me, the way the scales are removed from the eyes of infants born blind, and in the worst place in the world: in a concentration camp. In the Gurs camp, in southwestern France. Suddenly thanks to Paul a ball was no longer a ball, but pentagons and hexagons; the framework of the barracks was an equilateral triangle, the poorly designed doors were parallelograms instead of rectangles, and so on, and Paul guided us into this world of forms and numbers — I was just twenty, I was emerging from war, I'd been wounded; when I had just left the Spanish conflict, I was plunged back in, forced against my will, into the war a few months afterwards. Later on, in 1946, despite my age, in Germany, I enrolled in high school: I got my diploma as best I could. Then at university everything was different. The further along I got in my studies, the more adept I became at mathematics. I moved to West Germany. I was already too old to become a brilliant researcher. I was content to try to transmit this passion to high school students, then to university students. But I didn't rest until I found again the one who had revealed this path to me in the most terrible circumstances — finally this ended up occurring at the Warsaw Congress in 1983 (fine year that, 3 × 661, the first time the Congress took place in an odd year). I saw Paul Heudeber again there, forty years after Gurs. He had for some months been the director of the Mathematics Institute of the Academy of Sciences in the GDR. From that moment on we wrote to each other regularly. In our letters we talked about the camp, the camps (after Gurs and a number of military episodes I was interned in a Soviet camp); in his letters, Paul didn't hide the despair at everything that held him in its grip. Nor did he conceal what he called "the lessening of his mathematical appetence," which had led him to accept this employment rather than continue with his research. He had left to his student Helmut Koch (whom I glimpsed here this morning) the pursuit of his work on Galois groups and p-adic numbers. We wrote to each other two or three times a year until 1995. After 1991, he could no longer hide his political despair. The end of the GDR, but also the Yugoslav explosion made him mad with sorrow. *Humanity*, he said, *by gaining capitalism, seems to me to have lost humanity. Everywhere in the world.* War, violence, injustice. Antifascism opposed the horror and tried, as well as it could, to bring peace and justice to Earth. Even though I didn't share his views, I tried to lift his spirits by telling him that a new order would no doubt soon form again. His suicide in 1995 sadly showed how profound his depression was — but also that the trace of violence is never easily erased.

I had to interrupt, with perhaps a voice slightly more annoyed than I wanted it to be — excuse me, but there's nothing to prove that Paul Heudeber killed himself.

I'm sorry if I offended you, dear Madame, but there's hardly any doubt about that among the people with whom I associate (*the people with whom I associate,* good Lord, suddenly I could picture henchmen with soft hats and pistols in the pockets of their trench coats): Paul Heudeber put an end to his days out of despair, despair at the collapse of the Eastern Bloc, at the disappearance of his country, but also despair at the return of war in Europe, in the Balkans—he would also be devastated by today's terrible attacks in New York. He chose to put an end to everything because he couldn't bear this violence and because mathematics, which he told me had been a light in the darkness all his life, no longer really consoled him.

I thought for an instant about Maja, who had the luck to be snug in her cabin. Later, Jürgen Thiele revealed to me that this man's name was Isidro Baza, and that he had in fact been interned in the Gurs camp with my father; he had escaped at the same time as Paul, more or less, and after some time wandering, had found himself enlisted (by choice or compulsion, I have no idea) in God knows what Spanish legion, *on the wrong side.*

He was, moreover, right to think that Paul would have been extremely shocked by the September 11 attacks; I remember that when the war in Yugoslavia had begun and Germany, just recently reunified, had supported Croatian independence, Paul had raised his arms to heaven, shouting that it would set off a disaster and that at all costs Yugoslav unity must be reinforced, come hell or high water. Paul had just turned seventy-three, and was of course retired—they had kept his name somewhere in the organization of the new Institute, as an honorary member.

Hearing this Isidro Baza talking about the 1940s had made me realize that I'd almost never met a camp comrade of my father's—not any close friends, in any case. Aside from Walther Bartel, who was ten or fifteen years older, and who my father regularly spent time with, devotedly: he too was a fervent communist, often "under the Party's watchful eye," but never purged, unlike other communist colleagues from Buchenwald like Ernst Busse. Paul Heudeber was, however, active on the committee of victims of Nazism; he had always remained faithful to the Buchenwald Oath, but without—as far as I know—having any close friends with whom he could share these memories on a daily basis. Or perhaps he just never mentioned them to me.

Isidro Baza was continuing his soliloquy about my father. A sort of mystery emanated from him—why had he settled in Hanover, why hadn't he gone back to live in Spain?—his fidelity to Paul was also mysterious (not to mention his inflated self-esteem, which projected from his inordinate interest in my father), but I must admit that I was always mistrustful when it came to Paul's adulators, ever since adolescence: spending time in the GDR (and the political world in general) inoculated you against all forms of praise, which concealed either a ceremonial formality worthy of conferring an award or a funeral oration, or the monopolization, by the orator, of the qualities of the person whose praises he was singing, in an unbridled cannibalism of the other's merits, with all the glory returning, as a last resort, to the Party, the Organization, the Minister, *laudatio ejus manet in secula seculorum.*[*]

The Twin Towers had fallen a few hours earlier and in the belly of a boat moored to the shore of the Wannsee a few leagues before the Havel came to an end, an old teacher from Spain was praising Paul Heudeber and, apparently, was enthralling all those present—Alma Sejdić, the Bourbakists, the ex-Yugoslav logician, Robert Kant, Jürgen Thiele, everyone had little by little let themselves be hypnotized by this accent, at once gravelly and lilting, of the fractal specialist with facial hemiplegia.

It was probably cruel, but I was dreaming of taking refuge in my cabin like Maja or, even better, going to dinner, before it was too late, at the White Owl, alone facing the pewter candlesticks. I cite as evidence this rather desperate note in my journal, written on September 11, 2001 at midnight:

Horrible evening. Double disaster. Poor Papa, how sad all this is. I'm close to asking you to make room for me in your urn.

---

[*] "His praise remains forever and ever."—Trans.

XXIII

He lifted his hand toward the Black Rock at the top of the promontory to estimate its height, the top of an eroded peak, dark at
the lowest point, lost in the depths of wet foliage near a stream
that never ran dry, it leapt up to wear down the rocks, transform
them into pebbles, or into flat stones that could be warmed over
the fire and used as a stove, so smooth and so hard. The Black Rock
is a guardian of ruins, surrounded by walls, steps in stairways that
go nowhere, collapsed bastions that have become balconies over
the void and the dizzying, sheer drop of the cliff, lighthouses with
no lights. Ivy stalks and bramble thorns cling to the low walls and
hold up the last traces of buildings—a curved vault, its rear wall
reinforced by masses of fallen rocks, illuminates with its vestiges
the death of the citadel; once again he placed his rifle within arm's
reach against a rock, set down his bag next to the rifle. Sweat has
darkened his jacket with two long stains on the front, two black
tongues of pure effort, he uses the flask to drink some water from
the stream, it's still alive, burning cold.

The day after tomorrow you could be at the border, the path
climbs to the pass, will there be soldiers on this side, on the other,
the border doesn't signify much, it's a line between two forms of
misfortune,
   a dividing line,
   a divide,
   no doubt it will be goodbye rifle,
   goodbye cartridges,
   maybe even goodbye knife, goodbye gray gamebag, jacket,
boots, stench of shit,
   goodbye hatred,
   naked as if facing the Father.

He piles up memories, dry branches, and pinecones in a big heap in a corner between walls,

you make a pile,

the trout are lightning flashes out of the water, bright silver in the sun,

your father used to catch them like this, like a poacher, in the spring, when they circle around the rocks and eat grubs from the crumbling streambed, used to catch them by hand, using both hands while being careful not to cast any shadow on the fish, shadows betray, the sun blinds the trout with its glints, he used to catch them firmly and throw them onto the shore, they gleamed like flying fish, in the air, before struggling in the grass—your father would use a dirty cloth to hold the fish despite the slime and he'd stun it with a big blow against a tree trunk, the head would drip with blood, fish didn't have much blood the flesh was pink or white they bled little, much less than other animals and the movement of your father's arm with the trout in his hand had the same force, the same speed as his gesture when you got a huge slap, which threw you to the ground with half your face stinging, your ear red, your eye weeping: the trout would stop moving but you would get up again almost immediately, hand on your cheek. In the spring the streams coming down from the mountain are generous,

you've caught four fine trout,

you gutted them with the knife,

Thank you Lord, Lord you provide all things, Lord you ransomed us with your blood,

the Rock was steep and the climb took a long time, he'd had to walk around the peak and climb in the shadow, but then, at the top, in the ruins, he felt protected, surrounded—he decided to light a fire with dry branches and pinecones, invisible in full daylight, only the column of smoke could betray him, but from so far away it's almost impossible for anyone to see it—on the sloping ledge, around the ruins, heather and asphodel are growing; clematis climbs up the trees like a child, covering it in flowers; rosemary with its white and blue petals is advancing dizzyingly down the slope, with brambles and alder shoots, at the edge of the abyss as if about to dive. The donkey attacked the thick grass on the promontory, the couch grass on the banks of the stream where it drank for a long time; it managed to climb the side of the Black Rock, wheezing and whimpering, pausing, sometimes sideways across the slope, swaying its neck like a camel, he watched the donkey and wondered if it was going to collapse, but no, it held firm, and riding on its back the woman too held firm, sometimes she had to get down, she'd lean on the donkey as if on a staff so as not to put her leg on the ground, the leg with the splint—he carried the rifle, his game bag, his satchel, and the donkey carried the rest, the tin pot, the woman's pack, the packsaddle made into her saddle and every hour that passed, every combe they crossed, the blind donkey was on the point of stumbling, falling, it carried its mistress with desperate strength, its blind eye shone black and white, with force and hope, and the woman spoke into its ear, stroked it, encouraged it, gave it, at every pause, after water, one of her festive cakes, and the donkey moved forward,

you were also sweating as you climbed, weapon on your shoulder, you watched the donkey and the woman clinging to it, her right leg hanging down, trying not to set down her left foot, and that moving crutch, gray and fur-covered and one-eyed, brayed for a long time when the bend in the path was too steep, when the stones were too big on the track,

you gathered pinecones from the ground, you put them into the game bag, next to the dead fish; you also carried a bundle of heather under your left arm.

After they reached the top of the Black Rock, the woman, exhausted, sat down leaning against a wall, her leg outstretched, tears of pain in her eyes—he set up the fire in a sheltered corner, put down the stones, branches and pinecones; then he made an inspection of the ruins, gun in hand, an inspection of the tiny plateau, looking for traces of recent occupation; he found nothing, no cartridge cases, no remains of a fire, no trash. He only frightened a raven that flew off to join its fellows, cawing. He approached the dizzying northern escarpment; suddenly the sky isn't so clement anymore—bands of cottony clouds are climbing the valley from the sea; soon the fog will be upon them. He imagines people taking refuge here long ago, people from other eras, maybe even other languages, other beliefs, and, like him, watching enemies arriving from the valley—the enemy is the only certain thing. Over there in the distance, above a mountain, toward the border, a vulture is wheeling; it's a tiny black mark soaring above a carcass—man, horse, sheep—left to it by the wolves. A victim of a skirmish near the border, an animal fallen from a rock; the wind sweeps the combe and rises up to him, he feels it against his shoulders, his face. The sea is just forty or so kilometers away as the crow flies, but he feels as if he's in another world. Up until now they've been lucky not to meet anyone during the two days' journey in the mountain, no soldiers, no refugees, no deserters. No one.

The danger had been on the path up the slope,

the mountain is calm,

in wartime peasants hide, they're afraid for their herds, their wives, their harvests,

their secrets and their wells,

the mountain is calm, no sound of an engine, no truck, no shell whistling by, no gunshot ever since they left the cabin to climb northwards, no gunshot aside from his own to shoot a hare and two woodpigeons, too bad if he was heard. At the Black Rock, between the collapsed watchtowers, inside the ruined ramparts that vomit their red and white stones into steep piles, on top of this little summit, they are safe.

She can't manage to feel protected, not even in the heart of a remote fortress on top of a vertiginous peak, there is always the man, his knife and his rifle, he has made so many suffer,

why not me, he's carrying me off as an assurance of future pleasure,

the way you take your belongings with you, you protect them, watch over them, but what would have become of me without the donkey and him, he took care of me in his way, spared me, he knows I belong to him,

she bathed earlier in the stream, she found a hollow place, a hole in the hollow of the stream, where it was deep, she sat down in the delightful iciness of the stream, the man was further downstream fishing, she got completely undressed, naked, she wore only the splint he'd made for her, limping she sat down in the water that reached up to her shoulders, the current caressed the back of her neck, she could see the black and white saplings of her thighs in the water, her white belly, the black strip of her pubis, everything moved black and white with the current, her chest streaked with bruises, the water was absolutely freezing, she plunged in her head, immersed herself completely, she was trembling, her teeth chattered, she limped, slipped, crawled up to a big rock soaked in sunlight, she lay down on her back, the warm rock sweated sunlight; her belly, her chest reflected the sun—around her everything was rustling in the distance, God all creatures sing of Your glory, dazzled she closed her eyes, in the sun on the warm rock there was no more danger: the man, in the distance, busy with his duties, she was clothed in sunlight and modesty, she'd like to attain rest and confidence, get rid of fear and blemishes, images, visions, gazes, laughter, contempt, shame, everything she wanted to get rid of, memories she'd like to see dissolve in the light, vanish with the heat, finally,

where will I go after the border, I don't know anyone, I know names, after the border will I be returned to myself, will my wounds be erased,

I'll look for a place to heal, a place to get cured, a place of oblivion.

Her body is still battered, every gesture is still painful, lying on her back in the daylight she looks at the sheer cliff of Black Rock, up where the crow and vulture are wheeling, up where they could make a fire and rest in safety, God willing, she runs a hand through her short hair, it's just grown back an extra centimeter, feeling her

134

short hair makes her want to cry, brings back the shame and pain of crossing the village with everyone spitting at her, stripped naked by the enemy her left hand between her legs to hide her sex her right hand clutching her left shoulder to hide her breasts she could feel the shit streaming along her bare thigh, she could feel the shit tickling the inside of her knee, dripping down to her ankle, there were three of them walking up the village's main street before the eyes of all their neighbors and classmates and no one looked away, no one looked away when their hair had been cropped, when they'd been made to drink oil, when they'd been stripped naked, no one had looked away, people sniggered, men touched them as if they were objects, snatched at their breasts, hit them on their buttocks with sticks, the women had run out of tears, she remembers the noise of the clippers, like an insect, the monstrous clicking of an insect pulling your hair slightly and it falls, because the women were not on their side, not part of their world, because they were conquered without having fought, without any other dishonor, the uniform shirts the women had been wearing were torn off, the women had been beaten, had been made to drink oil, had been paraded like repugnant objects, like dogs or even worse, pigs, sheep after shearing, and the shit streamed out of them like shame, uncontrollably, they were foul tears of shit that fell on the shoes they'd been allowed to keep on while everyone laughed, and at every step there was laughter and insults, their bodies and their entire being were stolen by these cries of laughter and mockery and the mothers didn't hide their children's eyes, and the children laughed it was so funny to see these women go by the bakery all naked and shitting on themselves, the young men abused them, slapping their buttocks with sticks, you could sense they were aroused despite the shit and the misery, aroused by breasts and pubises, they lashed their thighs and hands to get a better look at what they were hiding and after they'd gone down the village's main street the women had been locked up in a corral adjoining a burned-down barn and were told people would be back to hose them down like the animals they were, that they were being purged so they could be inseminated with good semen afterwards, that they were being purged of the evil they had within themselves so they could then be filled with good sperm and their wombs filled with squealing creatures, a crowd of volunteers had been found willing to save the Homeland and the Race, and they had been thrown onto the straw in the corral, locked in, naked and stinking from the runs, their faces streaked with black tears,

all the sunlight in the world couldn't return my body to me—not the force of the lightning, or the rays of springtime, or the streams, nothing could return purity to me,

I don't know if the worst kind of stain is growing in my belly, this Rock so Black is only a pause on the path of evil.

The donkey is on the shore, it's eating wet grass, it's always anxious, it complains but it will carry me up to the citadel at the top of the peak, then it will carry me to the border, then where, tomorrow I'll be nineteen years old, no one knows, no one is nineteen in war, everyone is over a hundred years old in war, where is the man with the rifle, I'll go get dressed before he returns,

she regretfully leaves the flat rock and the sunlight; she hobbles over to her clothes and puts them on. The donkey nudges her with its muzzle, nestles its face in her breasts; she smiles and strokes its neck tenderly, it rubs against her, she scratches between its ears, it grunts in pleasure. She sits down to fasten the ties on her splint, strips of cut-up cloth that the water has distended. The ironmonger's son is a torturer and a brute who knows how to repair his playthings.

He climbed upstream along the bank, unobtrusively, in the shade, trout see danger even outside the water, they have good sight, they understand the movements of predators, of fishermen, you have to be unobtrusive to catch them by hand, three, he's already caught three, if you miss them they take cover under rocks where you have to go and flush them out, he climbs along the riverbank as quietly as possible: suddenly he glimpses the white flash of the naked woman on the rock, he turns his head away—he lies down in the grass, out of embarrassment, out of modesty, he lifts his face, the woman is a little upstream legs close together one arm under her head, she's dreaming with her eyes looking up at the sky, her skin is as white as milk, the tips of her breasts stand out from brown areolas, the single pistil of a blinding flower; the woman's body is gleaming from the stream water, her short, black hair still illuminates her face, by contrast; has she sensed his presence, she has placed her hand flat over the top of her pubis as if to hide its dark swell. He pictures himself stroking her suffering body in the cabin, her milky body, whose magnetic power he can perceive, more so as each moment passes. He contemplated her for a long time, the way you observe an insect in the grass, or a bird on a branch; he waited for her to stand up, for her silhouette to appear whole in the light, her chest in profile, so full, her round buttocks, he watched her hop over to her clothes, seeing her get dressed moved him even more than her nudity, the tenderness of cloth caressing her like a psalm,

a body that is no longer like other bodies, one you desire to be free of suffering, released from pain,

go back to your fish, go back to the stream,

he saw a trout on the bottom, a sandy clearing between stones, it spins round then freezes, fin in the current, it is greenish, with black spots, within his reach, he knows it will be slippery, that he has to aim carefully, try to place one hand on top, far up toward the head while the other joins it from below, the thumb quickly buries itself in the gill, that's the only way to grip it, the index finger too, in the sharp softness of the gill, with the other palm grasping the belly slippery with slime and with no hesitation pull the trout out of the water, rip it from the river, as soon as it's in the air it weighs nothing, it struggles, shines like a dark diamond in the sun, its skin seems brighter, more spotted, it beats its tail, slips, he pulls his hand back a little avoiding the dorsal fin and with an immense gesture, a gesture that is the whole universe, bellowing a harsh cry to the mountain, he smashes the fish's head against the bark of a pine tree.

He lit the fire in the corner of a crumbling wall, a wall of red-and-white rubble stones, rubble stones or bricks from long ago, he can't tell—the pinecones caught fire right away, then the branches, the heat from the flames disturbs the air, makes it wave in the sunlight, casts sparks skywards, crackling,

you've always loved fire, fire, bonfire, warmth, like salamanders and scorpions,

he placed the flat stones in the middle of the flames, when they're nice and hot he'll put the trout there, he's happy to feed the woman, to accompany her to the border, where exactly he has no idea, she is wild as a wild animal, he is surprised by her strength and determination, by her powerful will that is emerging as she recuperates, by her ability to walk all the way here, the more he looks at her the more he likes to look at her,

you'd also like to listen to her but she doesn't speak,

you heard her humming once, on the way, sitting on the donkey, she was singing a song in the donkey's ear,

she was singing a little girl's song to the donkey's immense hairy ear, she was overcome with brief incandescent bursts of joy, from time to time she'd sing to the donkey, she could sense her imminent release, the border is getting closer,

she realizes that the border is a kind of blossoming,

a passage and a transformation,

I know that soon I'll be far away and that only the memory of pain will remain, the scar, on my leg, within me the strength of lightning, its power, an inner fire,

leaning against this ancient wall, she watches the fire grow higher, she watches the man move about in front of the fire, he has put down his gun a few meters away, opposite her, in the other corner of this ruined room, he always leaves the breech open but there are cartridges in the chamber, she knows how to use that weapon,

if I leap up fast enough I can reach the rifle, cock it twice and shoot him in the back, at this distance I'll reach him and he'll collapse into the flames, he'll die shouting, and his hair will catch fire, and his horrible uniform jacket will catch fire, his eyes will end up exploding like the eyes of a lamb roasting on the spit and he'll stop shouting, overcome with one final convulsion before the ultimate immobility.

XXIV

It was Robert Kant's turn to speak, after the well-informed panegyric of Isidro Baza, Paul's friend about whom we knew nothing,
or almost nothing. Kant returned to his discovery of the *Conjectures*, and his publication of the translation of the theorem of twin
primes, which he called *Heudeber's theorem*. Everyone discovered
this demonstration, said Kant, after my article was published in
the *Journal of Mathematics*. Heudeber had followed in the footsteps of Emmy Noether; he had used tools of complex analysis
to demonstrate the infinity of twin primes, but he was moving
away from Riemann—in a letter to André Weil, Heudeber wrote:
The function $\zeta(x)$ is like a sun, it blinds us, absorbs everything. He
wanted to look past the sun. And he was right. When a friend
sent me the first edition of the *Conjectures*, on that cheap paper
the Akademie Verlag used, that dark cover, I couldn't believe my
eyes—at the time, scientific information took a while to travel the
globe; there had been rumors that a young German had demonstrated the infinity of twin prime numbers and had obtained many
other results, both in number theory and in complex analysis, but
that these studies were like seams in a deep mine, buried in the
middle of superfluous literary material: so no one had yet read
these studies when I opened the *Conjectures*. I wonder what this
is I'm reading, a kind of poem, an autobiographical narrative, in
which the mathematical research appears only much later on,
after fifty pages (fascinating as they are) of various considerations
in which math plays a marginal role. That's why I decided (after
writing to Paul to ask for his permission, of course, that was our
first epistolary exchange, dated 1948–1949) to translate and publish
the third chapter first. Translate, because I wanted people to be
able to read Paul's poetic texts, written in his beautifully formal

language, which had almost no need of translation. You all know the immense success of that publication, as well as its unsettling aspect for mathematicians who when it comes down to it are not very used to reading literature—today Heudeber is regarded as an exceptional mathematician. A slice of twentieth-century history.

I was listening to you, Professor Baza, talk about Paul Heudeber's *beautiful existence*, and how it takes on all its meaning with his death—as for me, I have the impression that almost the opposite is true, that Heudeber's death confuses the issue, that it concludes nothing, makes everything bigger, like a door suddenly opened: the month of November 1995 was a month of astonishment, of terror. The war was coming to its end in Bosnia; Radovan Karadžić and Ratko Mladić were accused of genocide; Israel was in shock after the assassination of Yitzhak Rabin; the mathematician Paul Heudeber died of drowning at the age of seventy-seven. I remember that page in the *Times*, that obituary written on the fly by a hack to whom Heudeber was above all a sycophant of East Germany, a communist writer-mathematician who had been in the camps and no one was sure if he'd committed suicide. Was it a suicide or wasn't it, that's what mattered in that article, and the taste for mystery that went with it—did Paul Heudeber follow the path of Jean Améry and Primo Lévi? I'm sorry, but the thing I found detestable, in the controversy that followed Heudeber's death, was to think that all camp prisoners had experienced the same thing, that they could be assigned the same kind of depression, the same taste for suicide. Buchenwald is not Auschwitz. Paul Heudeber's life in the camp was not Améry's. Many camp survivors suffered, are still suffering, but they don't kill themselves. Let's agree, for a moment, Kant went on, that he did commit suicide. *Let's make the supposition*, as he himself would have done in mathematical reasoning. What light would this suicide throw on his existence? Would it signify that he had been conquered? That he put an end to his days because he found himself in a fundamental impasse? What importance would *the world* have in that moment, so immersed in his solitary inner life?

It was hard for me to go on listening to Robert Kant. On the TV screen hanging from a pole mount on the wall in the *Beethoven's* ballroom, the Twin Towers kept falling over and over, the planes crashed into them from a different angle each time; on the bottom of the screen, a blue strip bore the red letters CNN LIVE, over the Stock Exchange quotes, the time, *Breaking News, George Bush has landed in Washington*, and the screen showed images of the streets of New York covered in dust, and the Pentagon in flames; I was half-listening to Baza's answer, *but Paul Heudeber's suicide would demonstrate precisely a total and absolute rejection of the world in which we live—it would transport Heudeber's whole existence into another dimension, like an entirely conscious translation of his essential trajectory toward* "elsewhere." Emotion, perhaps as much as his facial paralysis, was making him stammer—I was watching Robert Kant who was raising his eyes to heaven, a little outraged by Baza's speech. Curiously, it was the young Alma Sejdić who took the floor, and I wasn't sorry that she was managing to elbow her way to the fore and make herself heard in this battle of old men.

She had never met Paul Heudeber, she had arrived from Bosnia in 1994, seven years ago, she said, not long before Heudeber's death, and it was during the course of her studies that she had read *The Buchenwald Conjectures*, because her professor of complex analysis had quickly explained, at the beginning of a course devoted to Heudeber's theorem, that the *Conjectures* was a complete mathematical and literary mystery, which had to do with both poetry and *the secret music of mathematics*, and Alma Sejdić was fascinated by this secret music, she had rushed to the library to borrow this mysterious work and, she went on, she had discovered a text that was quite different from the one she expected to discover, such a concentration of pain and solitude, said Alma Sejdić, that even mathematics became frozen matter like stars, smooth and hard, and this violent solitude of torture and abandon, this almost absolute absence of love, aside from that external point that shines like Sirius whose ghost resounds over the whole complex plan, *this external point that is the unattainable woman*, said Alma Sejdić, this terrifying confinement under torture, reminded me of what I myself had experienced during the war (she looked straight at the ex-Yugoslav, who was nodding in virile compassion) and made me cry for days: thanks to the *Conjectures* I could look my trauma in the face, it had become an analyzable, external object, and I knew immediately that I wanted to pursue *these works*, that is, literary works, works in this particular branch of mathematics that is literature, and, more precisely, poetry, which is the algebra of literature.

Alma Sejdić had managed to make all those present smile, she had the same gift as Paul, the gift of imagination, of imaginative vision, and I was overcome with an immense affection for this young thirty-year-old woman who had torn herself away from violence and, like Isidro Baza, had persevered in mathematics thanks to Paul, thanks to the traces left by Paul—those traces had formed and transformed me too, and even today, twenty years after that catastrophe, while other catastrophes have occurred, while Iraq has burned, while Syria is destroyed, while the war is resuming at Europe's edges, I imagine Nasir al-Din Tusi considering irrational numbers after having seen Baghdad and Alamut burning, after having seen pyramids of skulls rising up in Baghdad: there are values that cannot be expressed as a relationship between two magnitudes, and they are innumerable. To be a historian of mathematics was, as Alma Sejdić said so eloquently, to pursue *these works*, story, poetry, and mathematics: Nasir al-Din Tusi was a theologian, a philosopher and an astronomer; from his observatory, he described the movements of the stars, the complexity of their orbits. He saw God in the elliptical, he glimpsed God in the clinamen between spheres and the musical play of the planets. Omar Khayyam explored the *jabr* and the positive roots of cubic polynomials, thanks to conics, to the intersection of hyperbolas or of parabolas—Khayyam was also a poet, he had written, not long after exploring the solutions to $a \times 3 = b \times 2 + c$:

> See these green leaves wet
> from a cloud's tears
> Drink the rosy wine,

for that is the custom of the wise.
Today this greenery
Is the delight of our eyes:
Whose eyes will take delight
in the green leaves where our bodies lie?

Walk, step*
I count one at each prime number of steps
I count one
I calculate $\pi(x)$ for x steps
Walk, step
I count $\pi(x)$ for x days
Euler is walking with me
I search for the smallest of the powers of infinity
The name of the last finitude is around me
I know the leap there is
Between the last finite thing and the first infinity
The sum of the inverses of numbers raised to the power n
Infinity in finitude
I walk
I add the infinitely small
I collapse
I walk
I add a fragment of infinitely small
I keep adding till I get to the ceiling
I walk in seclusion
The series of the inverses of prime numbers raised to the power
n advances in seclusion
Walk, step
The steps converge—
The steps converge and everything tends toward nothingness
Walk, step

* "Marche, pas": *pas*, which here means step or footstep, is also the particle
used to express the negative; there's a double entendre that's missing in the
English.—Trans.

Behind the decimal point of nothingness I count a prime number
of steps
I count the dead
I count the living
Walk, step
There are no people in numbers
There is nothing in calculations
Nothing in the real part
Nothing in whole numbers
And each second of my life
(Complex singularity)
Is in the language of pain
Imaginary part,
Walk, step
Blows
I count the blows
I count one at each prime number of the dead.

(Paul Heudeber, *The Ettersberg Conjectures*, Second Conjecture,
Corollary One, "Counting")

On September 11, 2001, when, like waves spreading on water, violence had shaken the boat *Beethoven* moored opposite Peacock Island, after everyone, at around 9 p.m., had half-heartedly (the unleashing of violence in the United States, on our television screen, and our suspended conference, had brought us all—Baza, Alma Sejdić, Jürgen Thiele, the Yugoslav logician, the Bourbakists, and me—so much closer together that we no longer wanted to separate) finally left the boat, some to get their bicycles and head toward the Nikolassee train station, others heading toward Potsdam, or still others, as in my case, going to the White Owl inn a few hundred meters away for a late, improvised dinner, which Jürgen Thiele had managed to obtain, despite the advanced hour, from the hotel kitchen.

I was realizing, as the hours went by, that new camera angles were being added to the continuous news loops, as if journalists were rushing all over New York to ask traumatized tourists: Did you by any chance, this morning at around nine o'clock, film the World Trade Center with your camcorder? Maybe even, the tiger of capitalism being so swift, the camera owners were lining up at the desks of news agencies to sell their most impressive images of sorrow and barbarism for a small fortune.

The Towers were also invading the restaurant dining room in the White Owl, via a television that, in the midst of this rather pretentious space (carpets, tablecloths, lace, candlesticks, waitresses with embroidered aprons), seemed to connote a tunnel in space-time joining Schinkel's early nineteenth-century Prussia with a futurist city in the grip of the Apocalypse. I didn't dare ask them to turn off the TV, but I took care to sit down with my back to the screen. By chance Robert Kant had preferred to stay on board the *Beethoven*, he wanted to go to bed, and listen to the radio, he explained. Kant had to take a plane to London the next day from Tegel, and was afraid it would be canceled, which was extremely likely: around us, everything seemed to be collapsing at the same time as the towers.

I had no desire to dine tête-a-tête with Jürgen Thiele, our tête-a-têtes were heavy with silence, dense with the unsaid; even though we always understood each other very well, perfectly even, our five minutes alone with each other on the deck of the riverboat an hour earlier had turned out to be sufficiently embarrassing for me to prefer to add additional company to this dinner, which in any case was nothing but a prolongation of the disaster. And so we asked Alma Sejdić to dine with us, and she happily accepted.

We were almost alone in the big dining room of the White Owl; one other table, far from us, a family with children, was finishing its meal. Jürgen Thiele had negotiated "a quick dinner," since the kitchen was about to close; I forget what we ordered—I remember, though, that after a swift, conniving look, like teenagers eager to get drunk, we had pounced on a bottle of white wine from the Rhine.

Outside the *Beethoven*'s atmosphere of mourning, after a glass of wine, I was overcome with a slight dizziness; the tension accumulated in the afternoon was escaping from me in whirling spirals. Jürgen Thiele was looking at me and smiling, Alma too had a benevolent look—the Ionian columns in the dining room, the Oriental carpets, the big curved bay window looking out onto the garden's darkness pierced, between shadows, by a reflection of the moon on the lake, all seemed so far from the words *Inn*, or *White Owl*, that even if that nocturnal raptor the color of snow had landed at that instant on Jürgen Thiele's shoulder, none of us would have thought it might be the mascot of the place. Alma Sejdić was a little intimidated; Thiele was bombarding her with questions about her impressions of this funereal day; I was observing the architectonic details, the elements of décor that Schinkel had used to give this room an aspect at once hieratic and timeless, rigid in its fluidity—everything fled to the rotunda and the garden. Everything fled: there was not a single right angle to keep the building from rushing outside; the columns, the elliptical apsidioles they demarcated, every shape was straining toward the lake, and I imagined that a couple dancing a waltz would have been guided by the room's architecture, without realizing it, toward the rotunda in front of the big bay window or, if the window had been open, toward the festooned terrace, which was a promontory highlighting the crinoline gowns and brocaded uniforms in the light of the lake. Overcome by drunkenness in a kind of imaginary dance, my eyes were spinning around the dining room of the White Owl and had completely stopped paying attention to the conversation: I was becoming liquefied, I was dissolving into a liquid as thick as the carpet. I was far away; a couple of dancers were whirling around in the center of the rotunda's ellipsis, neither inside, nor outside, in the exact spot where a halo of moonlight fell, light that I hadn't noticed before. They were handsome, she was tall, taller than her escort, sculptural, very dark; he was delicate, with fair skin, extremely careful with her, infinitely gentle; he would sometimes brush close to her, would place his cheek for an instant between her shoulder and neck, she would hold him close to her, for a second, before the movement of the music and their feet separated them. Jürgen was also fascinated; he was watching the man and woman dance and murmured to me: "They're dancing the dance of betrayal," but I didn't understand what he meant by that—did he recognize these people? It's a Yugoslav, or Hungarian, dance, the dance of betrayal, Alma explained. A dance of truth, of divination—by dancing, you discover what the other was hiding from you. There is nothing to conceal anymore, everything comes out in the open, everything is forgiven, without anything having to be confessed, that's the beauty of the dance of betrayal.

The couple glistened as if they were both wearing silvery lamé or were emerging from lustral water; the moon purified them of all lies. Alma was unstoppable: the dance of betrayal protects you from the shame of confession, it's a dance you must dance during times of change, during difficult times.

The man and woman were dancing the dance of betrayal before my eyes, there was more than one secret between them, they were holding each other close, whirling around, from shadow to light, I thought of Paul and Maja, of Maja's body, I imagined their own dance of betrayal—Schinkel's Berlin was mingled with ours, wild and uncertain; I could sense, see, glimpse a truth, a secret rising up between my father and my mother, it was I who had to dance the dance of betrayal, there was a river, a rock, an island between my mother and me, the couple stopped dancing, they were standing motionless, facing each other, Jürgen Thiele called me by my first name, Irina, Irina you were dozing off, and I opened my eyes, ashamed of having fallen asleep at table, ashamed it was in front of them.

Linden S. Pawley
Samsonville-Kerhonkson Road
Samsonville, NY 12461

Irina Heudeber
Schlossstrasse 26
12163 Berlin
Germany

Samsonville, May 27, 2012

Dearest Irina,

It's been over ten years since we saw each other, since that accursed day in 2001 and the panic that followed; you remember what happened and how that terrifying catastrophe broke my family—not so long ago I would have written "destroyed my family," which proves, perhaps, that I'm doing better, or that a part of the family did survive.

We are living as hermits now, Nelly and I, alone at the edge of these mountains where we can always convince ourselves that we're close to New York, a city we never actually visit.

A few days ago, I made the trip to Bryn Mawr College, just outside of Philadelphia; I wanted to spend some moments of reflection by Emmy Noether's memorial, in the old library's Cloisters. Of course I thought a lot about Paul, and about Maja. I'm sorry for my too-short, too-brief letter after Maja died. It's only today that I find the strength—the courage—to write to you at greater length, and no doubt the trip to Bryn Mawr and the minutes spent facing the simple plaque beneath the stone arches, which harbors the remains of Emmy Noether, were not for nothing: even if my work is celebrated all over the world today, I won't carry glory with me to the grave. No more than Emmy Noether, no more than Paul Heudeber did. So I can tarnish this glory a little in your eyes.

When Maja died, I couldn't find the courage to confront these memories; today I would like, as my life is finally reaching its end, to share them with you, dear Irina—secrets are never transmitted, they disappear with those who carry them. For once, I would like you to inherit them.

Your mother and I were very close, between 1964 and 1966, when I was living in Germany. We were practically living together, between Bonn and Göttingen. Maja was forty-six, I was forty-two. Paul had already stopped leaving East Berlin. He had almost stopped leaving his apartment. We never spoke about him. I didn't dare *think* about Paul, about the real Paul. Every day, or almost every day, Maja would receive a letter from Berlin. Every day she would smile at the letter as if Paul were facing her, would put it away in her bag and read it later, when she was alone. She often spoke of you, Irina, however—she spoke about your brilliant studies, your boarding school, the visits she made to you during vacations, when you were dividing your time between Berlin, at your father's place, and your mother in Bonn or Steglitz; I felt as if I knew you. Maja always had the irrational fear that you'd be regarded as a citizen of East Germany and that you wouldn't be allowed to return to the West.

In the GDR, those were the years of the economic boom, of freedom and passion. My research stay was incredibly fertile. I was trying to demonstrate the third conjecture in Paul's *Ettersberg Conjectures* and before I left Germany I had succeeded. It was this publication, in 1967, that earned me prizes and much praise. I was trying not to think about Paul, but I was walking in his footsteps and trying to resolve this problem that he had posed thirty years earlier, this intuition he'd had. I wasn't thinking of Paul, but I was pursuing his powerful mathematical thinking in the arms of the woman he loved. Paul was a sad genius. Dreamers like Paul, constructors of immense dreams, are always sad. Our world is not made for them.

Those two years with Maja were the most luminous in my life. Whatever Maja touched, even just with her eyes, became enchanted. She had such an aura, such magic—all those politicians around her had also fallen under her charm. She was very free. This freedom was fascinating. You loved her for this freedom and your immediate desire was to deprive her of it, to lock her away for love. The only person who had understood that was Paul. He didn't try to be near her. To live close to Maja was to know the hell of jealousy. To live close to Maja was to wonder every instant into whose arms you'd lose her. We were already older, in 1965, no longer in the prime of youth, quite the contrary, and yet every day I asked myself—who is that elegant man talking to her, standing in the middle of the restaurant? Who is that foreigner, like me, whose accent seems so charming to her? Who is that student staring at her like a miraculous icon suddenly weeping holy oil, with infinite surprise and absolute devotion? I would look at myself in the mirror, and ask myself, what does she see in me? She'll leave me, my elegance leaves much to be desired. She'll leave me, my German leaves much to be desired. She'll leave me, my intelligence leaves much to be desired. She'll leave me, I'm nothing but an American mathematics researcher. She'll leave me, my body is getting soft. She'll leave me, I am not Paul Heudeber.

Maja inspired me. I had to live up to her. I should thank Maja from the bottom of my heart; that jealous passion spurred me on to surpass myself. I was in better shape than I'd ever been before. I lifted weights. Ran. I wore a red silk ascot or an orange foulard tie. Sunglasses. A thin mustache. I drove a cute little "bathtub" Taunus P3; sometimes Maja deigned to get in and I'd take her for a ride. Sometimes I'd go for rides on my own. I was trying not to look like a math professor. Anything but that. I was a New Yorker, for god's sake! Not a little bespectacled math whiz. No. *Todo a lo grande.* I wanted to forget I was forty-two. The situation of German women was very different at that time, and Maja was an exception: a single mother, officially with a partner but not married, a women's rights activist, close to Willy Brandt since 1957, dividing her life between Bonn and West Berlin, a former Resistant who had spent the entire war in hiding in Belgium, she was utterly fascinating for a country where, in 1964, the German song in the running for Eurovision was called "Man Gewöhnt Sich So Schnell An Das Schöne" (We Get Used to Beauty So Quickly) and the refrain went:

Love, love, the most beautiful game of all
Never, never, will you have your fill

Maja adored that song.

It was the economic boom, Germany was importing Portuguese workers by the hundreds of thousands.

I was obsessed with Paul Heudeber. If I was passionate about Maja in this way, it was because behind her, there was the shadow of that Paul Heudeber, whom I had never met aside from in his work and texts. The madness of Paul Heudeber. The obsession of Paul Heudeber. I remember perfectly the first time I read *The Ettersberg Conjectures* in the partial translation by that poor Kant, published by the *Quarterly Journal of Mathematics* in Oxford in 1948. (I say "poor Kant," because he is completely, utterly, terribly lacking in genius, he's a clueless idiot). Kant had translated and commented on Paul's demonstration of the conjecture of the infinity of twin primes, which Paul had dedicated to Emmy Noether. What was strange is that Paul hadn't published it himself outside of that unclassifiable book that is the *Conjectures*. Of course he had no need of that parasite Kant. Kant quite simply put his own name to Paul's demonstration; under the pretext of translation (it's true, of course, there are poems on the strength of twins, on the infinity of infinities, and the magnificent text on whole numbers in the heart of the mathematical expositions), and he appropriated part of the prestige of that incredible discovery. Kant built his entire career on Paul's works.

The force, the implacable elegance, the formidable simplicity of Paul's mathematical writing, the lucidity of his reasoning, it made you want to cry. From happiness, but also, in my case, from jealousy. In 1948 I was twenty-six. I was beginning a thesis on number theory. I threw everything out. Paul Heudeber abandoned number theory after the *Conjectures*. He aimed instead for topology with this phrase, the last in the *Conjectures*: "How can we forget that stars are whole numbers—such darkness, the Universe that contains them!" I pictured Paul in Buchenwald, on the Ettersberg, beneath the uniform sky of Thuringia, looking for stars in numbers, in his head, in the power of his mind that resisted everything—imprisonment, pain, fear. Paul's mathematical skies struggled against violence. Yes, I had New York, the whole Columbia library, the cafés in the Village, the clubs in Harlem, and my thinking didn't amount to a tenth of Paul Heudeber's thinking in his utter destitution. Kant's article was full of euphemisms, "a mathematical work in extremely difficult conditions," that idiot Kant didn't even mention the name of Buchenwald, even though it was one of the few camps known throughout the whole world because of the images of the Weimar ladies forced by American soldiers to visit it, mid-April 1945, ladies who file past the piles of emaciated corpses, handkerchiefs to their noses, tears in their eyes. The trial of the camp's SS had been in all the papers in the spring of 1947, at the very time when Paul was publishing the *Conjectures* in Berlin. When I arrived in Germany in 1964, the Auschwitz trial was underway.

I met Maja because I was refused a visa to enter East Germany: I was supposed to meet Paul Heudeber, with whom I had been corresponding. I had learned enough German to read the *Conjectures*; I had defended my dissertation, published articles, I was benefiting from a grant for a year of research: I was going to demonstrate the third conjecture, the most incredible of them all, called the "conjecture of the space between prime numbers, or of multiple twinness," the first part of which Paul had demonstrated, that of the infinity of twin primes. I had an intuition, which turned out, after a long labor that lasted over a year, to be right. For Paul, it was the beginning of a long mathematical epic journey toward topology, the study of complex varieties, which would carry him to utopian spaces—he would become interested no longer in numbers but in *position*, that is, in form. For me, it would ensure me a guaranteed income among number theoreticians: Heudeber's Third Conjecture is now called Pawley's Theorem.

You already know all this, dear Irina, of course. Forgive me. I am aware that old age is softening my brain. Even though I have trouble remembering what I did yesterday, the months spent in Germany in the 1960s are extraordinarily close. I can see myself again in the Ford Taunus, with Maja; the gear shift was located on the steering wheel, and on the long single front seat, Maja could slide over to me and lean her head on my shoulder—we loved going for rides in this little automobile, between Göttingen and Bonn; we'd take the road south, via Marburg and Koblenz (I can see us again reaching the Rhine at Koblenz, how wonderful to drive alongside the river as it appeared and disappeared at the bends in the road, to gaze at the vines whose wine we'd drink during our rest stop), and once we went to Liège, I'd been invited to give a presentation at a conference, Maja accompanied me. I found the date in my notebooks: Thursday, October 6, 1966. It had been over twenty years since Maja had been back to Belgium. I had wanted to find out more about that part of her life (especially about Paul's life, why hide that).

I learned everything you know already: for a while, Paul and Maja contemplated fleeing Nazism to Austria, but the Anschluss made that plan impossible. Belgium isn't very far from Göttingen, and Paul set a lot of hope in the Belgian Communists in Liège, who at the time were governing the province along with the Social Democrats and were welcoming refugees with open arms. They easily found a smuggler in Aachen and reached Liège on foot, through the lush green hills scattered with black cows, in September 1938. They were in fact taken in by the local Communists and the aid networks of the little German-speaking community in Belgium. Paul had a contact at the University of Liège, a student of Hilbert and Emmy Noether, who helped Paul and Maja as much as he could. Paul was hoping he could give private math classes to survive. In October 1966, Maja showed me the house they lived in between 1938 and 1940, nestled in a little street on that large island in the Meuse the Liégeois call "the Outremeuse." My notebook mentions the Impasse Croctay, which, evidently, led to a street called Roture, where Maja and Paul had rented an attic room from a landlady whose name I've forgotten. The neighborhood was somber, low red brick houses, as if crushed by the setting—Maja told me they could barely stand upright in their bedroom, which moreover was almost completely lacking in comfort. She remembered the path to go to the bath house, at the end of the island . . . Paul was studying at the university library, thanks to the complicity of that student of Emmy's; he just had a few minutes' walk to go to the Faculty of Science where he would spend his days absorbed in mathematical periodicals and books.

It was strange for Maja to find herself, in my company, faced with these memories. She thought of Paul, of course; she seemed absorbed, at times far away. She didn't accompany me to the university for my talk, but went for a walk, to try to find, if possible, the city she had known; when I met up with her, that evening, at the hotel, she was already in bed, with the light off; I was sure she was pretending to sleep.

Love, love, the most beautiful game of all
Never, never, will you have your fill

Belgium was invaded on May 10, 1940; the fortresses everyone had believed were impregnable and which protected the Albert Canal fell on the 11th. On May 12, the Germans entered Liège. In the meantime, on May 10, Maja said, she was arrested at her home by the Belgian authorities along with five hundred other people, "enemy nationals" and far-left activists. Curiously, the fall of Liège and the installation of German authorities in the Palace of the Prince-Bishops on the 12th ensured that all those people were immediately freed—I went back to my attic, alone, Maja said: Paul was in Brussels for two days with some colleagues. Paul came back almost three months later—Maja learned that Paul had been arrested in Brussels with all the German nationals, most of them Jews or antifascists, who had then been evacuated to the South: Paul found himself interned in a camp in southwestern France. After the armistice, he managed to leave his prison and cross occupied France to rejoin Maja in Belgium.

Dear Irina, you know all this, of course.

During our visit to Liège, in 1966, it seemed to me that Maja was escaping from me into her memories, into the memory of Paul, who was very much alive in Berlin—I was waiting for the moment when Maja would say to me, Listen, I'm leaving, I'm going back to find Paul. Fortunately it wasn't simple, at the time, Paul was barricaded behind his antifascist wall and Berlin seemed very far away. We had planned to leave Liège two days later—I suggested to Maja that we leave the next day. We were having dinner in a brasserie in the center of town, on the Place Saint-Lambert; I remember candles and pewter candlesticks, Maja's face lit up, with a certain sadness in her eyes. Maja told me about the Resistance, the network she belonged to. After the raids on June 22, 1941 (the "summer solstice" operation, during which four hundred Communist activists were arrested by the Nazi secret police), Maja and Paul were forced to abandon their attic room and take refuge by going into hiding. They lived in sailors' lodgings on a canal boat called the *Angel Gabriel*, moored in the midst of boathouses and barges, on an island in the Meuse: sailors were comrades. All the canal boats and worksites around were more or less allies to the cause. But they still had to hide. Maja spoke better French than Paul, or rather she knew how to imitate a kind of Dutch accent that protected her from questioning. Paul spoke very little French, Maja told me. He just knew math terms. He could of course give a math class in French; he just couldn't buy bread without revealing that he was German. Without anyone wondering what this young German was doing there, without a uniform. Paul almost never left the canalboat. He would wait for Maja to come back, from her missions, her clandestine meetings ... He waited for her. He wrote. Actually *The Ettersberg Conjectures* began on that canalboat, you know—*The crocodile eyes of the Meuse are looking at me, the portholes are two half circles embracing a rectangle.* Alligators carry off their prey into the depths to drown them. The dream of demonstrating the twin prime conjecture began on the Meuse. Outside of time. Alone beneath the surface, in the company of fifty tons of coal or gravel.

Paul had a table facing the river, he observed the water, the boats passing by. He worked. The *Angel Gabriel*, the canalboat that housed Paul and Maja, bore a protective name. Despite the requisitions and confiscations Maja had a bicycle that allowed her to get to the center of Liège quite quickly. She would leave it in the courtyard of comrades who lived near their island. From there, you had to cross a footbridge, then walk as discreetly as possible along an embankment, hidden by silos and piles of sand, before you reached the *Angel Gabriel*. The boat smelled of damp and coal, said Maja. Paul would always leap up whenever I got home, said Maja. Contrary to orders, Paul never closed the doors—he'd go out and stroll on the deck, walk to the bow, would dream for a while gazing at the water, and when he was freezing (fall on the Meuse was ice-cold) he'd return to the stern and go back down to their lodging, forgetting to close the door behind him. Maja always surprised him—Paul was invariably sitting in the place where I'd left him, she said, always gnawing on his eternal wooden pencil. We were perfectly, selfishly, tragically happy. Ever since then, whenever, in Bonn or Berlin, I pass by moored canalboats, quite similar to ours, I feel a tightening in my chest.

Maja had tears in her eyes. The candlelight was reflected in the corners of her eyelids; her emotion only increased the beauty of her face and stirred the fire of my jealousy. Liège ardent city.

In September 1941, after the invasion of the USSR by the German army, the repression of communists, which spread to the Resistance, was intensified. They were sought out, spied on, arrested. Despite the Germanophobia, Maja managed to get accepted into the Walloon Front for the Liberation of Belgium, in which a number of leftist and communists of the Belgian Communist Party belonged. Perhaps it was the case that the more collaborators there were, the more Resistants there were—according to Maja, the province of Liège was of course a little collaborationist, but also immensely Resistant. At the end of autumn 1941, German secret police launched a new wave of arrests.

On Friday, December 5, 1941, the eve of St. Nicholas Day, Maja went into town to try to buy something out of the ordinary for Paul. She had a meeting with a comrade who could help her find a gift; as usual, Paul remained alone on board the *Angel Gabriel*.

In that Tivoli brasserie in 1964, between the candles and the sips of wine, her voice vibrant, her eyes staring at the little flame on one of the candlesticks, as if she weren't really speaking to me, Maja told me about Paul's arrest. How she knew the Gestapo was going to come arrest them. How afraid she was to come home and warn Paul, afraid of being arrested with him. Maja abandoned Paul. I betrayed him, she murmured without looking at me. That was why she hadn't returned to Liège since May 1945. Because she couldn't bear what she had done there.

An abyss of mystery was opening before me—that was the betrayal according to Maja. Abandoning Paul, feeling responsible for his arrest on the *Angel Gabriel*, his imprisonment in the citadel in Liège, his interrogation, his torture, his deportation to Buchenwald. I felt jealous. I don't know if I ever, for a single moment, had access to the real Maja—there was someone in her who existed only for your father. Me, I just had the crumbs, the body, a little affection that she left to me, a reward for a nice dog. I saw very clearly, in Liège, that Maja was not deceiving your father with me. We were not made of the same material, for her. Not the same nature. It made me mad with jealousy, love, anger; I showed off in front of her, blew my own trumpet, I interrupted her, in the middle of dinner, to tell her about my latest successes in math and how I was thinking I could succeed at demonstrating something that Paul, indeed, had glimpsed, but that he hadn't managed to prove. Maja was crying as she confessed to me that she had betrayed Paul and abandoned him to the Germans, deep down that didn't matter to me, it was her I wanted, not her old memories overflowing with guilt and with the genius of Paul Heudeber, scholar and martyr.

When we returned to the hotel, I thought she'd become mine again during intimacy—she refused me, turned to the wall, her back reflected a glacial sadness to me like a mirror. I knew now something that she couldn't tell anyone, aside from a foreigner like me, who would carry this secret to the other side of the world.

If there is a moment when my passion for her and, indirectly, for Paul, reached its height, it was during that evening in Liège.

Love, love, the most beautiful game of all
Never, never, will you have your fill

It was my duty to write to you. I know you're his daughter. That this story belongs to them, to her and your father.

The next morning, I drove very fast, between the hills of the countryside of Herve and Eupen, on the way back, to impress Maja, who hadn't opened her mouth since we woke up; she remained dreamy, leaning against the door, her hand in the grab handle over the window, I was listening to the engine, whenever the road climbed or twisted a little I'd downshift noisily, I'd take unknown curves at absurd speeds, teeth clenched. In Eupen, I decided to cut through the pine forest to a German village called Röntgen, like the physicist of the same name, there were no speed limits at the time in Europe, the "bathtub" Taunus was not at all a sports car, but on an impeccably straight forest road headed toward Germany, among the ruts, it became a sports car: from time to time I'd glance at Maja, she was clinging to the handle, silent, her jaw a little set, but with a slight, ironic smile, I wanted that half smile to stop, why, because she didn't love me enough, because I hadn't yet demonstrated anything, because I didn't reach as high as Paul's ankle, because I'd never reach anything at all, so I pressed my foot on the accelerator of that ridiculous engine of the European car the Germans had the nerve to call a Ford Taunus, a narrow engine full of clicking sounds with the voice of a soprano whose countless baubles vibrated in unison, the road that was not a road supposedly led to a customs post in the middle of the woods, in the shadow of the firs, the Taunus leapt forward ever faster, at every jolt a tire skidded, both my hands were clutching the steering wheel, my fingers squeezed tight as if over the object of my passion, I couldn't know what speed we were traveling at, I didn't want to lower my eyes to the speedometer, my only glances, few and swift, were to observe Maja, a quarter of a second, her profile, her face from the side, her nose, her long hand on the handle: she could sense something was happening, that it was time for something, she said nothing, her lips remained closed, she looked at the road, the Taunus bounced in the ruts as if it were going to fall to pieces, Maja still said nothing, my foot was all the way down to the floor, the Ford couldn't go any faster, the trees became a green mass, a continuum of ferns and fear, at the next jolt we went off the road, my hands hurt I was squeezing the steering wheel so hard, Maja remained silent, clinging to her door, Maja remained silent, I finally slowed down, we reached a crossroads, I braked, the old heap turned a little sideways and I collapsed in tears over the dashboard.

Maja didn't move, she didn't wrap her arms around me as she used to, she didn't try to comfort me. An hour and a half later we rejoined the Rhine, and thirty minutes after that we had reached Bonn. I dropped Maja off at her place, she got out of the Ford, reached for her bag. She didn't invite me in.

I set off again for Göttingen.

Dear Irina, don't judge me. Don't judge us. It seemed important to me to write to you, before everything ends in oblivion.

I didn't see Maja again until September 10, 2001, almost thirty-five years later. My daughter died on the morning of the 11th in the most horrible way, the day after our reunion. I sometimes feel as if all of this is connected, obscurely, that we're all connected to each other like a series of numbers, even though we don't really understand how.

Very sincerely,
Linden Pawley.

In the wooden house called the Nikolskoy House, the log cabin at the edge of the forest, straight out of a Russian fairytale, a Berlin transposition of Gorky's house in Nizhny Novgorod or of the dachas from long ago by the frozen sea near Petersburg, but on the Wannsee, a stone's throw away from the place where, in days gone by (over ten years ago) the *Beethoven* of sad memory was moored, not long after receiving the letter from Linden Pawley, I was having lunch, in mid-June 2012, with Jürgen Thiele. Our relationship had ended a few years earlier in boredom and a slightly disgusted chastity that had degenerated into a kind of weary but powerful friendship, which made it so that we were always happy to see each other again, at least for the first two hours: then his character ended up, as always, exasperating me, and I was very happy to go back to my place, alone. At the Nikolskoy House, he had of course forgotten to make a reservation, and despite the weather, which was magnificent that day, we had to eat inside, so I started out in a bad mood.

Jürgen Thiele said he was sorry a thousand times, and ordered two glasses of champagne to earn my forgiveness, which, I must say, worked.

The Havel was a flow of molten metal; the sun was setting fire to the end of Peacock Island and Sacrow on the opposite shore.

The Nikolskoy log cabin had so to speak been imported from Russia—built in the early nineteenth century by the King of Prussia to honor his son-in-law, the future Tsar Nicholas I, so that he wouldn't feel too homesick. It had gotten through the world war without any damage. The walls were made of impressive logs; the windows decorated with triangular panels of larch, with an openwork of carved flowers in the most Russian taste. You really felt, surrounded by all this wood, that you were lunching in the heart of Siberia.

I didn't really know how to approach the subject that was obsessing me; I remember waiting until the very end of the meal (strawberries!—strawberries from Werder! Jürgen Thiele exclaimed, almost like a child) to tell him about the contents of Pawley's letter. At the mere mention of his name, Thiele's face clouded over with sorrow; the horrible death of Pawley's daughter in the collapse of the Twin Towers (her body had of course never been found; she was identified months later from a few fragments) had remained a terrible shock. Jürgen may be clumsy and absent-minded, but he is also quite perceptive; he managed to get me to talk. I couldn't manage to say the words. Linden was my mother's lover. Finally I whispered the phrase without giving it flesh, because it made no sense to me, "my mother's lover."

Despite their large age difference, Jürgen Thiele had been very close to Paul. His student, then one of his closest friends.

His face didn't change at this revelation. The dimple on his square chin didn't start trembling, his eyebrows didn't go up, his mouth didn't open wide. I would never have thought of Paul talking with Thiele about Maja's affairs.

And yet.

Men, men, men.

I told Jürgen everything. Paul's arrest, Pawley's Ford Taunus. All of it.

Paul spoke often about the *Angel Gabriel* canalboat, Jürgen Thiele replied. He idealized that period in his life, those few months in Liège between arrests. He wrote, he worked, he was in love. One day he saw, instead of Maja, the Gestapo arriving. As he writes in *The Buchenwald Conjectures: Today, I'm surprised by their gentleness.* He is surprised, looking back, by the gentleness of the Nazis. They come instead of Maja. Paul knew that Maja could have saved him. Paul knew that she had chosen not to do so. Paul knew that Maja had preferred to see him arrested instead of taking the risk of her own capture, or placing the entire network at risk.

Paul could talk under torture, he didn't know much; it was a different matter for Maja. Paul was happy she had made this choice. Maja's choice ennobled her, he said. He had nothing to forgive, he said. He ... he loved your mother—and Maja loved him too, beyond what was reasonable, I think.

And Jürgen Thiele fell silent then, out of modesty, because he didn't want to give me the impression that he knew my parents better than I did.

I found this attentiveness touching. Of course I was wrong. I imagined that *beyond what was reasonable* meant: after Linden Pawley.

I changed the subject. I had opened a door that could lead only to us, to our history, I've always hated this meaning of the word "history." *To have a history.* I sensed that Jürgen had wanted to talk about me. About him and me. I watched him eat his strawberries. He licked his mustache, looking so pleased with his strawberries from Werder. I shouldn't have drunk that champagne, I too should have ordered strawberries from Werder, in the park of the palace in Sacrow, on the other side of the river, there is an age-old oak tree— or rather, the ruin of an oak tree, an immense but maimed tree, as if hit by lightning. Goethe's tree too, in Buchenwald, burned during the bombardment of 1944. The Sacrow palace was transformed by Schinkel, you know, the architect. The Sacrow palace was lived in by that poet friend of Hoffmann, I forget his name, a French name, you know?* In the Sacrow palace, they say, Mendelssohn composed his string quartet in A minor, you know, the one that goes *ta, laa, ta, laa* that devastating melody at the beginning of the andante,

I had to stop contemplating the Havel, I could feel tears appearing at the corners of my eyes.

* Probably Jean Paul.—Trans.

Maja my love,

Mathematics is a veil draped over the world, it takes on the shapes of the world, to envelop it completely; it's language and matter, words in a hand, lips on a shoulder; mathematics rips itself off with a swift gesture: then you can see the reality of the universe, you can caress it like a plaster model, with its rough edges, its hills, its lines, whether they're lines of flight or life lines. This veil, this cloth over the world, is also the shroud in which I wrap myself when the time to leave approaches—the sheet that will cloak me, the paper that will cover me over, the ghost that will survive me, I know its fibers, its weft, I can describe the landscape it forms, discover its accidents, glimpse the radiation it emits and even its secret spectra. I can say: Maja, your beloved skin, each pore has its singularity, and you, sleepless equation, love without resolution, I look at the sea and I wait for you. Oh I know, time has passed, places, horrors, revolts, imprisonments, liberations, sighs, joys, threats, fears.

I look at the sea and I wait.

I am old. Elderly. I love this warm water that so quickly becomes deep and ice-cold, by surprise, as its color changes, from emerald green to turquoise then dark blue. It took forty years but here the fascists have finally been conquered. Or rather dissolved in money the way weapons are dissolved by rust. No more Wehrmacht uniforms, no more torture. In the corner of my rocky beach there's a tall pine, some Scotch broom with no flowers, some bay laurel—nature vibrates, it smells of thyme and Apollo.

I seek solitude. I don't mingle with the crowd. My body still allows me to walk (to find a deserted beach: it's not hard in the middle of autumn) and to swim (so as not to think about anything).

The waitress at breakfast tells me it's exceptionally warm for the season, so warm that the hotel will stay open until December 8.

To be alone in such nature is an immense pleasure. I write this letter sitting on a big rock which probably belonged to the ramparts of a Greek colony.

I look at the sea and I wait.

Maja, now that nothing keeps us from living together anymore, we are attached to our solitudes. These last few months, these last few years spent with each other in Pankow showed me not just the pleasure there was in sharing our little sorrows and our readings but also the difficulty of frictions, of daily upsets. Sometimes I'm even relieved when you go back to Steglitz, which makes me terribly angry with myself—how could I no longer want what I've desired for so long? Irina would say that I am *terribly stubborn*, obstinate, pigheaded, but that's not true. I'm just persistent.

I try to remain sincere with us. We must keep ourselves in the realm of the exceptional. Maintain ourselves in the absolutely perfect. Not to last just for the sake of lasting. Mistrust the desire to last. Said the seventy-seven year old man.

Cicadas look like very big flies, they strike cymbals located under their abdomens when the temperature goes above 73, 74 degrees Fahrenheit. They sing, apparently. They play these cymbals a hundred times a second until they obtain that strident modulation. The Latin name for cicada is *Lyristes plebejus*, which I'd translate freely as "the lyre player of the lower classes" or more precisely "the musician of the proletariat." Only the male cicadas sing. They sing to attract the females. They don't stop. You could say that I have the constancy of a musician of the proletariat. Cicadas feed by pricking branches (of pines or olive trees) to suck out the sap. At the moment, they're supposed to be dying, already dead even: according to my little manual of Mediterranean botany and entomology, they don't survive past October. They're like the hotel, they close for the winter; this year they've decided to prolong the season a little.

Maja, I feel as if life has sided against me, on a number of points;

my theorems have been refuted, some of my conjectures have been contradicted, many of my works have already been forgotten; we will no longer construct Socialism and I will no longer be called "comrade"—we are paying the price for our intransigence, our mistakes, and our too great submission to Russian warmongering. I was, perhaps, wrong to believe, to conjecture, that humanity was made for peace, sharing, and fraternity.

I look at the sea and I wait.

I look at the sea, it's the opposite of war but transports it: over there, past Italy, they're still fighting in Bosnia, even though peace is close. Over there, there was horrible warfare, concentration camps, genocide. The sea could transmit shouts, vibrations, radio waves so powerful you'd see them on the surface of the water, you could read them, you could make out the names of the dead, you could join them by swimming. In this beautiful hotel, with these tourist companions whom I don't know, whom I encounter at breakfast, to whom I address a polite greeting at dinner, I try to forget tragedies and war crimes. I warm my old bones in the autumn sun. Sometimes I tell myself that you should've come with me—and immediately I change my mind, we would have squabbled about everything.

Maja, I can't manage to forget the April ceremony in Weimar. (I can't even manage to write *Buchenwald*.) The reunions with a thousand old camp companions. The speeches. The implacable speech of Jorge Semprún: *The time has come to be done with the rhetoric and the mythologies of a pseudouniversalist party spirit*. I'd have liked to shout: Those mythologies are not criminal, they fought for us and with us, they fought the SS, fascism, they gave us the strength to organize in detention, to liberate ourselves on our own—and in the end it's for their sake we were sent to the camps. Should we really abandon all of that? Close Buchenwald in on itself? Shut the aberration? Going back to Buchenwald is not the same as turning your back on Buchenwald. I cannot say goodbye to the Ettersberg. The camp is inside me. I could quote hundreds of phrases, by Celan, Améry, Levi. *I know what not returning means*. But the experience of the camp vanishes. Its very trace in writing becomes illegible with time. Dozens of testimonies have been published, in all the languages of the camp. What will it be like in twenty, thirty years, when the authors of these testimonies have all died? I fell silent.

I look at the sea and I wait.

The pine is leaning over the rock as if over a shoulder, as if it wanted to look at its face in the water; a light wind from the north has risen. In early April 1945, there still weren't any leaves on the trees of Ettersberg. The nights were always freezing. We were hungrier than ever. The little camp was overflowing with thousands of poor guys who had "survived" all the evacuations of nearby or distant camps. They were dying of typhus, dysentery, and starvation, by the hundreds. In my bursar's office I didn't abandon my numbers. I thought of you, of Liège, of the *Angel Gabriel* canalboat, I wondered if you'd ended up being arrested also, if you were in a camp, somewhere, I hoped you were free, fighting alongside our Belgian comrades, gun in hand. Sometimes I dreamed while awake—I imagined it was you who were coming to free us, that we were leaving together, you and me. The bombing of the camp in August 1944 had shown us what German cities were undergoing—we felt an awful mixture of joy, fear, and sorrow at this. Let them burn us all! Let's be finished with it, in a dawn of fire!

That April ceremony in Weimar, returning to the camp, curiously brought that terrible feeling back to my throat. In Buchenwald, the barracks are destroyed, the little camp no longer exists; the bunker, though, is still there; tourists visit the cells where comrades were tortured and killed, as today I look at the ruins of this ancient Greek colony without understanding them, without them provoking anything in me except a form of indifference transformed into an aesthetic sensation. I envy Irina and the historians: Auschwitz, Buchenwald, Dachau, Mauthausen are nothing now but museums. Museums of what? Is it me they're looking at in this museum?

The Mediterranean is so gentle, it's hard to think that here too people are exterminating others, here too people have exterminated others, that thousands of people have lost their lives, planes, cannons, bayonets. This immense bay furrowed by the wake of boats goes almost as far as France. Gurs is on the other side of the Pyrénées, far to the west, it seems to me. I'm not even sure if there is a museum there—I won't go to check.

Over fifty years later, I still dream about the Ettersberg. Obscure dreams, full of fear, pursuit, hunger, death, torture. In these nightmares there are unknown faces, barracks I don't recognize. Is my unconscious creating its own camp? Do our dreams have a better memory than we do?

A family has just arrived to set themselves up on the sandy part, in the center of my little beach; a woman, a man, a child, a parasol. I can see us again soon after Irina's birth, do you remember, at that time crossing Berlin meant avoiding the ruins, juggling with destroyed railroad tracks to get to the Zeuthen lake, forget the city and its mountains of rubble for a while.

Maybe this family has nothing to forget, though, maybe sitting on this beach is only a continuation of their happiness—the child is walking naked in the sand, he or she is playing with a plastic rake, the father scoops the child up like a package to take it to the water, the father gets a volley of blows from the rake in his legs in protest, he shouts and abruptly flings the child into the water, the mother gets up to rush to the kid's aid, the father holds his knee laughing, it looks like the child too is laughing and splashing everyone while continuing to strike the water like Ulysses himself in his boat. Distance prevents me from making out what language they're speaking.

If we could relive x moment in our life, I would choose a day with Irina when she was little, all three of us, by the edge of the lake in Hankels Ablage—do you remember that scandal, in the early 1950s, the stray bullets of the American soldiers training ended up on the Wannsee beach? A girl had almost died, her throat hit by a projectile. In Miesdorf-on-SBZ* we didn't run the risk of American bullets, just bird shit—I remember we went out in a

* *Sowjetische Besatzungszone:* Soviet Occupation Zone.—Trans.

boat all afternoon; we took turns rowing, facing each other; Irina was in either my arms or yours. She fell asleep, woke up, fell asleep again. The lake was as dazzling as the Mediterranean is today. We picnicked on the water, in the middle of the circle of boats, then we drank a beer at dinner, on land, on the magnificent terrace at Hankels Ablage, Irina still in our arms, before spending the little money we had to sleep on site, in that hotel that was anything but luxurious—baby Irina between us in that tiny bed, impossible to close my eyes, I spent the night musing seated by the window, looking at the moon on the lake and listening to you sleep. I could see your leg emerging from the sheet, Irina was sleeping on your belly, head between your breasts, as if she had just been born. Life could have stopped there. That night, six or seven years after my liberation, when I truly realized I was finally out of the camp, when the war was over, when I had a child, a job. A hope.

Maja, you know, before, moments of happiness had been very brief—hiding in Göttingen, hiding in Liège in that impossible attic, hiding on the *Angel Gabriel* ... Then, moving to Berlin, the labyrinth of rented rooms and landladies, there was Rixdorf, Gesundbrunnen, Kreuzberg, others I forget. Here, facing the Mediterranean, Berlin is too far away for me to remember them all.

You and Irina will remain like the suns in the cold that's coming closer.

I look at the sea and I wait to close for the winter.

XXV

Slime, ashes, blood: he tries to wash his hands as well as he can with earth and a little water after the trout have cooked on the burning stones, the earth showing between the rocks is red, crumbly, sandy.

He brings lunch to the woman sitting in the corner of a ruined wall,

Lord, preserve us from evil,

None of the women he has killed or penetrated ever moved him so, he knows her face now, her short hair, soft as fur underhand, her milk-white skin, her marble breasts turning pink in the center, her most secret odor, of saffron and valerian, her breath and the perfume of her breath,

you miss the intimacy in the cabin,

the gentleness of the coma,

you offer her meal to her on a stone dish,

you opened up the fish with the knife,

you removed the skeleton,

she recoils a little when he approaches, a reflex of fear, she knows what they say about the man with the knife, the man with the stick, the man with the rifle,

she knows him,

I've seen him already in other men,

I know those hands, that beard, those gray pants, that stench of the barracks,

that overzealous sweat, that breath,

I look around the Mountain to avoid his gaze, when he comes toward me,

I'm not fast enough to take his rifle and kill him,

not agile enough,

in my bags there's a weapon,
a long, thin blade like a knitting needle,
so pointed at its tip,
I'll hide it in my blouse,
if he comes in the evening or at night I'll pierce one of his eyes
with it, the tip will bury itself into his brain and he'll collapse.
Tomorrow or the day after I'll reach the border,
the donkey will carry me,
the sky is suddenly a cauldron of clouds, a bag of cotton: the
sun has disappeared behind the mountain, milky cumulus are
passing over the Black Rock, swift, humid fog.

XXVI

I arrived at Weimar on Thursday, April 7, 2022, at around 4 p.m. A white veil was blanketing the sky from Berlin; I remember being cold during the transfer, at Erfurt, on the platform. A Russian missile had fallen on the Karamatorsk train station in Ukraine; they counted over fifty dead among the civilians who were trying to flee the Donetsk oblast—in Weimar there was a fine drizzle.

Luckily the weather forecast for the next few days was favorable, if not actually pleasant.

I took a taxi from the train station to the Ettersburg Castle hotel, on the Ettersberg. Seven or eight kilometers away from the center of Weimar. The taxi followed the road that a thousand inhabitants of the city, men and women, on April 16, 1945, constrained and forced, on orders of General Patton, had taken on foot, to go to Buchenwald, finally to open their eyes to the hell they had lived alongside without seeing it for over seven years, accompanied by American soldiers. Patton himself had visited the camp on April 15 and, if we are to believe the accounts at the time, had hidden himself to vomit. The camp had been freed for four days.

Sick people, corpses, skeletons; lampshades made of human skin for lamps that diffused only the black light of cruelty, the heads of Polish prisoners shrunken by hatred and the techniques of the Shuar Indians.

The inhabitants of Weimar fainted.

I know that Paul left Buchenwald on April 16, 1945, so he could have seen the column of civilians, the women in knee-length skirts, the men (most of them elderly) in jackets and ties, climbing up to the Ettersberg, with their picnics, as if it were a springtime excursion. It was nice out, they say. In images from the time we see men in suspenders wiping their foreheads, some women in blouses and others in heavy wool coats. In the forest, on the road that leads to Buchenwald, some smile at the camera.

My father went back to Göttingen, where he found his sisters again, after 130 kilometers on foot and a pause in his native village of Gernrode where he and his comrades (four of them left the camp together) were so afraid of being lynched by the frightened old men that they preferred to sleep in an abandoned stable rather than knock on closed doors in the twilight. The allied troops had passed that way a week earlier and were speeding toward the Elbe where they were supposed to join with the Soviets.

My Aunt Ilse (her husband, a prisoner in France, wouldn't return until months later) did not recognize Paul when he appeared; at least that's how the family legend describes his return—my father had no memory of this detail, of not being recognized: he remembers raiding my aunt's meager wartime pantry.

What I know of the last days in Buchenwald I read in books. My father never told me about the liberation, or about the anxiety about the possible evacuations of the camp by the SS, or about the attempts at "negotiation" with camp authorities so they would "forget" for a few days the order to evacuate and massacre the inmates. My father's name appears, as far as I know, in a single book of testimonials, that's all; he is described, by a Czech fellow inmate, as a friendly, daydreaming young communist, on the quiet side.

The castle, now the Schloss Ettersburg hotel, is a Baroque affair, a hunting pavilion built in the early eighteenth century—with a courtyard, a church with a beautiful belltower and outbuildings. In the late eighteenth century, the place was swarming with artists—prose writers, poets, musicians, painters—from Weimar and the brilliant court of Duchess Anna Amalia of Brunswick, duchess of Saxe, Eisenach, and Weimar. Goethe, of course, but also Wieland, Herder, and the musician and actress Corona Schröter belonged to the *Nation of Ettersburg Castle*. A theater was built on the ground floor; *Iphigenia in Tauris* was performed there in the summer of 1779. Duke Karl August hunted roe deer and fallow bucks in the forest. Between May and June 1800, to isolate himself, Friedrich Schiller settled on the castle's third floor; despite the cold and the frequent visits from Goethe, he managed to complete his play *Mary Stuart* there. In 1808, during the Congress of Erfurt when Czar Alexander met with Napoleon, imperial hunts were organized on the Ettersberg, which involved the deaths of dozens of mammals—deer, fallow deer, white-tailed deer—and feathered animals, pheasants, and partridges, perhaps as many dead animals as soldiers fallen in the Battle of Jena.

The theater was transformed into a Weapons Room.

Today, after having been a retirement home in the already ancient days of East Germany, the castle, entirely renovated, has become a hotel—the baroque facade repainted a rather cheerful yellow; a very beautiful English-style park, on the southern side of the castle, has opened a meadow below the castle's terrace, which seems to climb to infinity between the trees, like a causeway to heaven, for absent giants.

In the southeast, three kilometers away and 120 meters higher up, hidden by the forest, almost at the top of the Ettersberg, is the camp of Buchenwald.

The proximity of things suffocates me—Weimar two hours from Berlin by train, the concentration camp a forty-five-minute walk for Goethe, Schiller, and me.

The receptionist is very young and friendly. She shows me around the hotel—dining room, breakfast room—you're out of luck, she says as she hands me a blue brochure, you're leaving before our next concert, Sunday at eight—we're also organizing some *cultural activities*. The blue brochure announced the list of activities of this *cultural refuge* that had been the Castle on the Ettersberg.

My room is modern and functional; it is located in the part called the "old castle." High ceiling, furniture made of dark wood—I'm immediately reassured, No, Madame, this is not Schiller's bedroom.

What remains from yesterday aside from the worst?

My phone gives me live news of the destruction and death in Ukraine. The Russians claim they are fighting once again against the Nazis. The nationalist Ukrainian far right clings to the name of Stepan Bandera.

The most violent German far right exists again.

The chain-rattling of these ghosts terrifies me.

On Sunday, people flowed in to Weimar to celebrate seventy-seven years since the liberation of Buchenwald. On Sunday, April 10, at 3 p.m., on the *Appellplatz* there will be speeches, and extracts from the Buchenwald Oath will be read. I was lucky to get a room, the receptionist tells me. We were lucky not to be interned in Buchenwald, too. This phrase does not pass my lips. I'm mad at myself for being in such a bad mood with this poor young woman who has done nothing to me.

In my bag I have a copy of the dossier compiled by the security services of the State of East Germany on Maja Scharnhorst. Printed, in a cardboard file folder, old-style. Pieces. Scraps, from bags containing millions of destroyed papers; pages reconstituted fragment by fragment by students and then by computers, Artificial Intelligence. In my bag I have my mother's life, in pieces and seen by the Stasi. I have just turned seventy-one (I can't believe it myself) and I'm going to read the secret file of my mother, who died over fifteen years ago.

More chains rattling, more ghosts.

Paul had read his own file after the fall of the Wall, a few years before his death—he had laughed a lot, because his cardboard sleeve was far from empty, but for him it was empty of meaning: true, it contained several hundred pages, the transcriptions of telephone conversations, copies of many of his letters, notices about his comings and goings, surveillance reports during his trips abroad, dozens of reports on his scientific activities, Party evaluations, etc.—the traces of intense administrative activity, but nothing that interested Paul. True, he learned that one of his neighbors in his apartment building kindly informed the Stasi about his visitors and friends, but that was such common practice, it was such a cliché of the time that he wasn't even upset. Paul was more horrified by the language of the Stasi than by the reality of facts about him. The hundreds of abstruse abbreviations, jargon, bureaucratic expressions, made this reading extremely difficult. Paul had asked for a copy of a single report (he had to pay for the photocopies, obviously infuriating him, the Federal Republic exploits the communist people to the very end, the GDR is getting revenge with photocopies), which made him laugh till he cried. Paul had read it to us out loud, this text, he was laughing so hard he could never manage to get to the end, he had to pause to breathe, to spit, to cry—his face was lit up by joy, my father's eyes were laughing, but they laughed as I'd never seen him laugh before, with his copies of two typewritten pages, his fingers near the little black dots, memory of the holes for ring binders, he read and tried to say as quickly as possible the endless socialist acronyms in the preamble,

Surveillance observations of Prot. BDPOGH *of KWH meeting of the second account of* ISS-SectionIII / Teil2. IMS HA II/3 For *vor-W.*

And Paul would start laughing, his hands would tremble, the sheets of paper would tremble: it was a report of the meeting of a scientific committee in the late 1960s of the Science Institute (Paul hadn't managed to remember *who* among those present might have churned out this report). What made him so happy was that they understood nothing, nothing, nothing at all: the writer of the report, who obviously was neither a mathematician nor a physicist himself, was trying as hard as he could to recount a conversation about which he had understood absolutely nothing, and it was *hilarious*, according to Paul, *hilarious and depressing*: I understand why the Socialist camp collapsed, he said, laughing. The verbatim account of the meeting was full of remarks in brackets [*Inadequate mathematical observations*] that became increasingly numerous, the informant revealing himself to be ever more bewildered by the discussions of the specialists present: the functionaries who had "dealt with" the source must have realized

that their "informant" hadn't understood a word, and that conse-
quently, they didn't either.

Paul, however, had noticed some "blanks" in his file: it mentioned Maja Scharnhorst often, of course—interactions with Maja
Scharnhorst, conversations, letters, trips with Maja. But about
Maja herself, there was no mention: Paul's file made a number
of references to the HVA, the external secret intelligence branch
of the Stasi, which concerned itself mainly with West Germany.

Maja had also requested her file, as every citizen had a right to
do: they had replied (at least this is what she told Paul and me)
that her HVA file did not exist, that there was no longer a file
under the name of Maja Scharnhorst. Which, given her political
activities and her history, was absolutely impossible. So this file
had been destroyed, like many files of people in the West, in 1989.
Perhaps the remains of these documents could be found among
the fifty million archival pages destroyed at the end of the GDR,
millions of pages that ended up filling some sixteen thousand
bags of pieces of paper, which they were going to try, whatever
the cost, to reconstitute.

When Maja told me this, that "the affair of the bags" was well-
known and that an initial estimate of the time it would take to
patch together *by hand* the destroyed documents had reached a
period of time approaching that of a trip to Pluto on a bicycle,
I immediately thought of Iran and the Ayatollah Khomeini: the
land of Tusi and of Khayyam, born respectively in Tous, in the
suburb of Mashhad, and in Nishapur, a few parasangs to the south,
or a week on horseback from Tehran, was also that of the Islamic
Revolution of 1979.

In Tehran, in the building of the former American Embassy,
"students aligned with Imam Khomeini" patiently reconstituted,
for months, the documents that American diplomats had put
through the shredder. Photographs of the time in fact show young
people in classrooms (the building that housed the American
Embassy in Tehran looks a lot like a high school) in the process
of juxtaposing strips of two-millimeter-wide paper to restore their

contents; all the documents thus obtained were published by these "students aligned with the Imam" and books on the clandestine activities of the Great Satan in Iran were sold on site, in the former embassy transformed into a museum "of pride and shame."

It would have been nice to transform the building in Lichtenberg in Berlin into a Museum of Pride and Shame: today it's just a "Stasi Museum," with no students gluing together torn pieces of paper.

Over thirty years after the end of East Germany, I obtained a copy of my mother's file—computers or small hands succeeded in reconstituting what the Stasi knew about Maja. Those who insinuate that it was better to wait as long as possible before making these documents accessible because of their potentially incendiary content are malicious gossips, slanderers.

Chains, ghosts.

Irina, your father is dead. That's what Maja told me on the telephone, Irina, Paul is dead, as if she were telling it to herself, trying convince herself of it. His body had been found, drowned, a week after he hadn't come back to sleep in his hotel room. No one knew exactly what time, or even what day, he died. The circumstances are even less clear. I went to Girona where his corpse was kept and to Barcelona where the consulate helped me carry out the legal formalities concerning, I quote, the expatriation of the body. On one hand they were repatriating him, on the other they were expatriating him. The dead travel even less easily than the living. A few days after the funeral (Maja had taken charge of its organization, personally I thought there were too many people) I went to his home in Pankow, at 32 Elsa-Brändström-Strasse, at the corner of Trelleborger Street.

Having arrived in front of the building, I greeted, as I do every time, the elephant on the facade—a bas-relief dating back to the 1920s, placed just above the entrance door; an elephant passing in profile, to the left, between the curve of the doorframe and the window of the stairway. A rather gentle elephant, with a long trunk, fine tusks. I climbed up to the third floor. Paul Heudeber had been renting this apartment since 1953. In the southern part of Pankow, not far indeed from the ruling circles of the GDR, but not nearby either. His position, all his life.

I wandered around the apartment as I waited for the movers. There were boxes of math books with gray bindings, works by Marx and Sartre, novels by Alfred Döblin, Christa Wolf, Günter Grass. A gilt bronze Eiffel Tower. Photos of Maja, of me. Some hats. Everything was already arranged into piles and categories; the scientific manuscripts would join the collections in the Institute's library;

Maja wanted to keep some of his things, I wanted to keep others; I had set aside a few souvenirs for those close to him, Wolf Biermann's CD *Chausseestrasse 131* for Jürgen Thiele, for example. Most of the objects and furniture would go God knows where, with the movers. I realized to what extent, aside from the rather impressive quantity of papers (correspondence, rough drafts) my father had lived in a kind of austere simplicity—most of the furniture dated from the 1950s; he hadn't encumbered himself with anything.

I wondered if one arranged one's apartment specially when one decides to end things; if one left clues, traces. When my father chose to spend a month on the Catalan coast, did he know he would not come back? I couldn't manage to remember the precise moment when he said goodbye to me. To me it hadn't seemed like a permanent farewell.

The movers arrived. In no time at all the apartment was empty. Curiously the only thing that remained was the gray rotary phone, placed directly on the parquet floor—the telephone was such a precious, rare object in East Germany, I thought. I considered carrying away the telephone, it was ridiculous, I had no use for it—and also it belonged to the State. No, not the State anymore, the Company.

I shut the door behind me, went down the stairs, reached the street, said goodbye to the elephant, went to have a coffee at the bakery that had just opened next door.

When I was little, I would always ask Paul why there was an elephant sculpted above the door of the apartment building; Papa would reply:

"This building was built with money from the sale of the tusks of elephants hunted at night around Weissensee by the prestigious Imaginary Hunting Society of Pankow. We must pay homage to the animal who allows us to have a roof over our heads."

I would sigh, and insist: Come on, why is it really? And Paul would find a much finer reason, if not more valid:

"It's to signal to passersby that this building and its inhabitants have the strength of the phalanstery; that we are moving stubbornly toward utopia."

XXVII

This time he knows. Hears—he hears. He presses his palm hard over the woman's mouth. Her eyes open wide, looking at him with fear, he places a finger across his lips. Silence won't save them. She has understood, she also heard. Rattling and voices.

The Black Rock is a labyrinth of collapsed walls where fog and fear slip through.

The sun has gone behind the mountains, absent shadows leave their phosphorescence on the stones, the plants are black with terror, she can perceive the sounds of men, heavy, the noises of soldiers, dull and clanking, the voices of soldiers, self-confident, how many are there,

he has gone off holding his rifle,

she gathers herself into a corner where no light reaches, she has her bags with her, the donkey is grazing somewhere,

she listens,

a crow croaks,

the crow is warning its fellows about the presence of men,

some songbirds are calling to each other, looking for each other in the springtime,

a titmouse is singing, its voice is smothered by human phrases, too far away for her to understand them, voices dulled by stones, stony voices, men talking to each other,

she listens, some disputes, shouts, the sounds of weapons, a gun explodes in the evening and echoes through the mountainside, the detonation eddies around the Black Rock, birds fly up, wings clack,

she hears the donkey braying,

she hears a second gunshot,

she hears the voice of the deserter,

over there, on the left,

he is not shouting.

Shadows are overtaking everything, the lower part of the walls are already in darkness,

I'll curl up in the dark until I disappear, and when daylight comes they'll already be gone,

she knows that's not what will happen,

there is no star in the sky and she senses that these voices that are combining are combining against her, that no one is on her side, that her side does not exist, if she wasn't wounded she could have tried to flee, descend the long steep path with the taste of abyss and sweat,

my heart, it is echoing its machine-gun beat through the whole mountain my mouth is dry, I'm cold, ever since the beginning of the war I've been cold, months and months of cold, I'll leave for the north to escape the freezing cold of the sea, of the city, of the country, the women who were with me that day didn't want to leave, they paid, they said, they paid with their bodies and their shame they paid they can stay, stay shorn, stay raped, stay soiled, stay in the stable, in the intense cold of the stable, the absolute cold of war that will last for years to come, at night, in everyone's sleep, torturers and tortured,

I can't stay in the cold of war, even if it means dying here at the Black Rock, in this old castle, this ancient trace of soldiers we know nothing about, if they were victorious or vanquished, if they ever fought in these regions, so close to the border,

I feel the man's desire,

always his desire for possession in his caresses, his touches, he touched my thigh, took care of it,

before the war he was a poor guy in a family of poor guys, from the very first day of the war he carried a weapon, the very first day,

without a uniform he was already carrying a weapon,

from the first dawn along with others he battered people to death,

from the first ray of sunlight they were loaded onto trucks,

from the first evening they killed as a unit.

Before being chased by the movement of war,
to the other side of the moving line of war.
The front twisted and contorted like a wounded person in pain
on the ground,
the front was advances and retreats,
the front was calm, silent defeats, then sudden defeats,
then collapse, resumption,
captured and recaptured I collapsed in the straw in the stable,
I hid my shaved hair under a scarf and I asked the lame donkey
to accompany me northwards,
where everyone had already gone,
to get crushed against the border like your nose against a shop
window,
as children, we'd breathe
to draw opaque clouds on the glass.
And now I hear the voice of the weapon that will finish me off
after holding me hostage for a few days,
the voice of the weapon that has just killed the donkey,
the voice of soldiers who are asking the deserter what he has
to offer in exchange for his life,
I am exchangeable goods,
I have hidden the long steel needle between the dressing and
the splint,
I will die killing.

He surprised the soldiers leaping from the half light, in the faded
light of dusk, gun aimed at them, there are three of them,
they are your age, wear your gray uniform,
without insignias,
they are deserters, they too want to cross the border tomorrow,
they recognize each other, don't know each other, fraternize
mistrustfully, one of the soldiers suddenly shoulders his rifle, aims
into the night past one of the walls and shoots,
a horse, or a calf, what luck,
the donkey started braying,

it's a donkey, idiot, it's my donkey,
the soldiers look at him, what are you doing with a donkey,
another soldier approaches the wall, shoulders and shoots,
stop idiot you'll wake the whole valley,
I'll shoot if I want to, there's no one in this valley apart from
three peasants, some horses, and vultures,
what do you have aside from a donkey and a rifle?
He is silent, he knows he's going to have to share if he doesn't
want to lose everything,
share or kill,
that's what his war experience tells him.
He'll have to be wily to evade the fire of three guns. Join forces.
He looks carefully at their faces, one has pale eyes, smooth,
black hair, stuck on his forehead by filth, prominent cheekbones,
absent lips, scarcely a line between nose and chin, a short week-
long beard; his uniform is almost new, the leather of his gun strap
shines on his shoulder, the barrel of his rifle doesn't have a scratch,
he hasn't fought, what is he fleeing—the second is short, thick,
his face looks crushed, too wide, the Lord's hand flattened it when
he came out of the womb, he stinks of stupidity and brutality, he's
the one who fired the second shot, his jacket is dirty, spotted with
oil, his hands are black with grease, he's a mechanic or a driver,
the third is thinner, younger maybe, his face is gentle, his eyes are
too, his cheeks are round, his hair blond.
The wind started blowing,
they are in freezing clouds, they'll light a fire,
the young babyface sets up a bonfire in a corner of the wall as
he himself did a few hours before,
flames spray the blackness, sparks are carried by the wind and
gush into the night like tracers,
he hesitates to tell them about the woman, he hesitates but they
can discover her so easily,
he speaks of the woman to the three soldiers, Lord have pity,
may He order it so that His angels will protect you,

*

She heard his voice betraying her. She doesn't know if she should crawl, try to crawl to run away, she has understood that the donkey died from the soldier's bullets, she is ready to die too but before that she will kill, savagely she will kill one of the soldiers, she is suffocating in fear and the freezing humidity of the Black Rock, there is no sky, she hears no bird, no creature of any hope, that's how she knows the war is lost.

Everything goes too quickly.

I've suffered more than I've lived, springtime is opening onto the winter of hatred and death.

She lets herself be dragged by her arms on the ground to the room where they lit their fire, like a branch or booty,

watching the flames he crouches, leaning on his rifle, the three soldiers have thrown all their wood onto the fire, the lights leap higher than the walls of the red and white bricks, build a new space, a cell of light for a new torture,

you watch the three soldiers get excited at their discovery, rejoice at their luck,

the mechanic is rubbing his greasy hands together, his eyes would light a bonfire, his mouth is drooling as if he were in front of some roast meat,

they have torn off her shirt,

the woman's white skin is rippled with amber from desire and fire,

the bruises,

I hide my breasts with my left arm they don't see the splint I rest my right hand on my hip,

the skirt is lifted over my legs, they want to see, they're not talking anymore they're grunting,

the soldier with the pale eyes and absent lips lifts the skirt with the barrel of his rifle as if he was afraid, he is afraid,

the young one with the pink cheeks has a desiring mouth, incredulous hands, clumsy feet,

you're crouching behind them rifle in your hands you could kill the woman with a bullet in the head at this distance so she wouldn't suffer, you could leave and sink into the night so as not to see, walk far away so as not to hear, you could reach the border alone,

the woman's body sullied and strangled will be left to the vultures,

in the early morning a red fox will come, it will sniff the naked corpse, bite the flesh from the side, the immense plume of its tail will be radiant from the dawn, hunger will urge it to rip apart the tenderest pieces, to cover its fangs with blood barely congealed,

it too will forget itself in the pleasure of devouring,

the soldier with the pale eyes and absent lips has lifted the skirt with the barrel of his rifle up to the woman's sex, she is groaning, tears of rage are shining in the reflection of the flames that are not dying down,

she holds down her skirt with the hand that was hiding her breasts,

the young soldier looks immense he wants to lay his immense shadow on the pale woman and despite himself leans forward,

nothing more can be heard,

only the woman's groaning and the wood catching fire,

nothing more can be heard,

only the drooling noises of the mechanic and the murmuring shadow of the young soldier,

the soldier with the pale eyes and absent lips has leaned over the woman, he has stretched out next to her,

you will kill the woman,

I am the light of the world,

he that followeth me shall not walk in darkness, but shall have the light of life,

Lord receive this woman have pity on me and you take your rifle no one hears the sound of it being loaded, the wind is blowing and is raising tempests of sparks and glints,

I wrap my right arm around the soldier's neck, his face is not far from mine, he is smiling, the face with the almost absent lips and the pale eyes is smiling he has his hand between my legs suddenly

I shout for courage and strength, the needle comes up so quickly it scarcely has time to shine in the flames, it penetrates from bottom to top, it sinks in so easily, I hold the soldier's chest against me with my arm, an atrocious shout comes out of his mouth, a reddish slime streams from his pale eye and the needle goes deeper, I hear a shot, a fall, I hear a second shot and darkness happens, darkness happens, the light fades and I think I've fainted but the shouting doesn't stop even though the needle has penetrated his eye with its entire bloody length.

He took the mechanic's body out of the fire, its face burnt; the flames grew again, their light invaded the room open to the sky, with no other stars than the embers, he pulled the woman toward him, helped her put on her shirt, covered her with the uniform jacket of a dead man, she was shaking. He moved the corpses outside of the walls, trying not to notice either the punctured eye or the final force that made it burst open. He recovered the weapons, the ammunition, the kits, found a nice flask of white brandy and military bread; he gave half of the bread to the woman, with some water. He helped her move, she did her business crouching down, hidden by her skirt. A few hours later, when the silence was as complete as the wind and night birds allowed, the donkey climbed up the slope of the Black Rock to its mistress; she had tears of joy, stroked it, bandaged it as well as she could.

In the meantime, he hid himself away under the absent stars and emptied the white brandy, in little swigs, until he fell into a somber sleep, populated with corpses and carrion feeders of every kind.

XXVIII

I got out of the bus at the Wieland-Herder stop.

I walked.

Friedrich Schiller, who had recently received the right to call himself Friedrich *von* Schiller and the letter of ennoblement that officialized this right, acquired for himself and his family in Weimar the pretty yellow two-story house one sees at the side of this most civil esplanade, planted with beech trees, where it looks so pleasant to stroll from bookstore to bookstore or have a coffee at the many outdoor cafés that take advantage of the absence of motor vehicles to extend their seating out into the street. The houses around also seem to be from the same era, the eighteenth century, and it's likely that aside from the trees, nothing has changed since the time when Wolfie Goethe came to ring the door of his friend Friedrich to suggest they go to the tavern, or climb up to the Ettersberg with him—if indeed there was a doorbell (I realize that I am absolutely incapable of walking in a city without trying to slice it into temporal strata and read it like a history book) at the time. Schiller must have been happy in Weimar. He was supported by the authorities, he had friends there. During one month he had written *Mary Stuart* at the Ettersburg Castle, then finished, this time at his desk, *The Bride of Messina, William Tell,* and just before his death from tuberculosis, in May 1805, his translation of *Phèdre* by the Frenchman Jean Racine. I read in a tourist brochure from the Weimar Classic Foundation that Schiller is a hydra, he possesses several skulls today (the most famous being the one Goethe contemplated in 1826, which he describes in a famous poem, and which he kept at home, under a glass cloche, nicely arranged on a blue felt cushion) and despite the efforts of specialists to put some order into this funereal profusion, no one knows, even today, which of these skeletal remains actually belong to Schiller; the research was abandoned, apparently, a dozen years ago.

Russia threatened to bomb Kiev again, almost 10,000 people died in Mariupol according to the mayor of the city, the main part of which is in the hands of Russian troops and Wagner paramilitaries.

Last night, at the Ettersburg Hotel, I read the contents of Maja's file. The information from the Stasi. My mother's lies, typed up by HVA functionaries. The information she transmitted until 1985—I didn't read any further. In the beginning, tears of rage, a desolate sadness, an absolute solitude—I couldn't think any more, I watched the clients and employees go to and fro in the castle's courtyard. I didn't resume reading until much later, almost the middle of the night, the moon was illuminating the opposite wing of the little castle between clouds. All our life was there, in papers hastily destroyed and patiently reconstituted. What we had experienced. The calm, easy life of my mother. The ease with which I visited him in the East as a child, then a teenager, then an adult. My father's exit visas for the West, for Paris, for London. His telephone line, his apartment, his official mail, all the things she'd obtained for him. For me.

The long investigation she had been the object of in the West, the way the HVA had protected her, their own suspicions, the possibility she was a double agent, the Stasi's fear that she was one—the risk was worth taking.

Where are the truths in a life of illusions?

In my own naivety.

In Jürgen Thiele's half hints.

In my mother's guilt.

What Paul knew. What he had forgiven. What he didn't want to see.

At around five in the morning, my past lay strewn in ruins on the parquet floor of the hotel room, that beautiful German room with such a high ceiling and such a narrow bed.

Dawn didn't come.

I spent an hour snoozing in the bathtub; boiling hot, I let the water slowly grow cold. I was red and wrinkled.

I went down to breakfast, made myself a nice sandwich in a roll, layers of smoked ham, cheese, lettuce, hardboiled egg, and I abandoned it on the plate. Even coffee disgusted me. I went out, walked at random, happened upon a bus that was leaving for the center of Weimar.

I got on without a ticket. All my life I've hated traveling without a ticket when circumstances forced me to. Illegal passenger.

I reached the large square not far from the Frauenplan and the Goethe House. At the Herder-Wieland stop.

I walked along the Ilm and went through the park without seeing anything around me. My memories were contaminated, I no longer knew if I should recognize what there was around me, trees, monuments, historical places; the quatrains of Khayyam were contaminated, the poems in Arabic and Persian that Goethe had loved, everything was moth-eaten, crammed, impregnated with lies. What I had always seen in the texts was now eating away at me, I could feel my legs, my crotch, my belly being pierced with holes, wounds, I was dissolving into the falsehoods and no truth, like Weimar all around me, was left to me.

The Russians bombed I don't know what I don't know where and people died, my phone tells me.

I reached the yellow house of Schiller. The author who greeted the new century just before dying.

I drank a coffee at one of those pleasant outdoor cafés.

I decided to climb on foot from the center of town to the Ettersburg Castle Hotel; my phone, between alerts on the situation in Ukraine, told me it would be about a two hour climb through the forest, with a total difference in height of 277 meters, 193 meters up and then a descent of 83 meters: three prime numbers. Auspicious. I'm in pretty good shape for my age, my doctor and friends tell me. I passed by the statue of Goethe and Schiller shaking hands, continued straight to the middle of the Bauhaus Museum, and crossed the railroad tracks.

In 1942, the director of the Museums in Weimar, with the approval of the Mayor, decided to arrange for the protection of the prestigious collections from the different historical places in the city, in case of air raids. The Archeology Museum, Museum of Fine Arts, Goethe's and Schiller's Houses. He had the idea of ordering wooden crates from the Buchenwald concentration camp, up there in the forest, which had a woodworking workshop and a whole beech grove at its disposal. Forty large wooden cases to pack furniture and books from the Schiller House, the Goethe House, and collections from the Museum of Ancient History.

The director also wanted to commission Buchenwald to make copies of furniture in the room on the top floor of the Schiller House: Schiller's deathbed, the desk on which he wrote, the spinet on which he played dances by Haydn, as well as one armchair per floor. All these pieces of furniture were loaded into a truck and entrusted the SS to have copies made. Schiller's desk and Haydn's *Dances* were thus locked up at Buchenwald and inmates were put to work to copy them. They had to find prisoners who were not just cabinetmakers, but also a piano-maker for the spinet—the whole world was at Buchenwald, and the copies were perfect.

On October 19, 1943, Schiller's desk was back at Weimar.

So Schiller didn't completely escape the concentration camp. He stayed there too.

I imagine my father in 1942 writing a part of his *Conjectures* in Buchenwald on Schiller's desk, the real or fake one. Paul Heudeber sitting there where Schiller had written *William Tell*, that story about a fight for freedom, against injustice. The replicas of the furniture, the desk, the spinet and the armchairs, are today in the Buchenwald Museum. Everything is contaminated by lies.

After an hour's climb, already worn out and out of breath, I reached a crossroads—an obelisk was erected at the juncture of two roads: on the right, the road goes back down to the Ettersburg. On the left begins the Road of Blood, the one that leads to Buchenwald, the road of death that prisoners were forced to build themselves.

I sat down on one of the flagstones at the corner of the pink granite obelisk and thought for a moment about Egypt, about Aswan, about the unfinished obelisk of Syene, still lying in its quarry.

I hesitated for many minutes about which direction to take and, after having a little difficulty getting up, I set off toward the Camp.

New Directions Paperbooks — a partial listing

*BILINGUAL EDITION

For a complete listing, request a free catalog from New Directions, 80 8th Avenue, New York, NY 10011
or visit us online at **ndbooks.com**